# THE GAP INTO CONFLICT:
# THE REAL STORY

OTHER BOOKS
BY STEPHEN R. DONALDSON


THE CHRONICLES OF THOMAS COVENANT
Book One: Lord Foul's Bane
Book Two: The Illearth War
Book Three: The Power That Preserves

THE SECOND CHRONICLES OF
THOMAS COVENANT
Book One: The Wounded Land
Book Two: The One Tree
Book Three: White Gold Wielder

DAUGHTER OF REGALS AND OTHER TALES

MORDANT'S NEED
Volume One: The Mirror of Her Dreams
Volume Two: A Man Rides Through

# STEPHEN R. DONALDSON

THE GAP INTO CONFLICT:

# THE REAL STORY

BANTAM BOOKS

NEW YORK • TORONTO • LONDON • SYDNEY • AUCKLAND

THE GAP INTO CONFLICT:
THE REAL STORY
A Bantam Spectra Book / February 1991

*Library of Congress Cataloging-in-Publication Data*
Donaldson, Stephen R.
  The gap into conflict: The real story : a novel / by
  Stephen R. Donaldson.
    p.  cm.
  ISBN 0-553-07173-4
  I. Title.
PS3554.0469R4   1991
813'.54—dc20                                    90-39569
                                                    CIP

Published simultaneously in the United States and Canada

Bantam Books are published by Bantam Books, a division of Bantam Doubleday Dell Publishing Group, Inc. Its trademark, con-
sisting of the words "Bantam Books" and the portrayal of a rooster,
is Registered in U.S. Patent and Trademark Office and in other
countries. Marca Registrada. Bantam Books, 666 Fifth Avenue,
New York, New York 10103.

Printed in the United States of America

BVG   0 9 8 7 6 5 4 3 2 1

# THE GAP INTO CONFLICT: THE REAL STORY

# CHAPTER 1

**M**ost of the crowd at Mallorys Bar & Sleep over in Delta Sector had no idea what was really going on. As far as they were concerned, it was just another example of animal passion, men and women driven together by lust—the kind of thing everybody understood, or at least dreamed about. The only uncommon feature was that in this case the passion included some common sense. Only a few people knew there was more to it.

Curiosity wasn't a survival trait in DelSec; it certainly wasn't the pleasure it might have been in Alpha, Com-Mine Station's alternative entertainment/lodging Sector. Laidover miners, discredited asteroid pilots, drunks and dreamers, and a number of men who never admitted to being ore pirates—the people who either didn't fit or weren't welcome in Alpha—all had learned incuriosity the hard way. They considered themselves too smart to ask the wrong questions in the wrong places, to notice the wrong things at the wrong times. None of them wanted trouble.

For them, the story was basically simple.

It began when Morn Hyland came into Mallorys with Angus Thermopyle.

Those two called attention to themselves because they obviously didn't belong together. Except for her ill-fitting and outdated shipsuit, which she must have scrounged from someone else's locker, she was gorgeous, with a body that made drunks groan in lost yearning and a pale, delicate beauty of face that twisted dreamers' hearts. In contrast, he was dark and disreputable, probably the most disreputable man who still had docking-rights at the Station. His swarthy features were broad and stretched, a frog-face with stiff whiskers and streaks of grease. Between his powerful arms and scrawny legs, his middle bulged like a tire, inflated with bile and malice.

In fact, no one knew how he had been able to keep his docking-rights—or his tincan freighter, for that matter—as long as he had. According to his reputation, anyone who ever became his companion, crew, or enemy ended up either dead or in lockup. Most people who knew him predicted he would end up that way himself—dead, or in lockup until he rotted.

He and Morn looked so grotesque together she staying with him despite the clear disgust on her face, he ordering her around like a slavey while his yellowish eyes gleamed that none of the men nearby could resist a little harmless scheming, a bit of gap-eyed speculation. If I could get her away from him— If she were mine— But the story was just beginning. No one was surprised by the nearly tangible current which sparked across the crowd when she and Nick Succorso spotted each other for the first time.

In a number of ways, Nick Succorso was the most desirable

man in DelSec. He had his own ship, a sleek little frigate with a gap drive and an experienced crew. He had the kind of piratical reputation that allowed him to seem bold rather than bloodthirsty. His personal magnetism made men do what he asked and women offer what he wanted. And the only flaws in his cavalier handsomeness were the scars under his eyes, the cuts which underlined everything he saw and grew dark whenever he saw something he intended to have. Some people said he'd inflicted those cuts himself, just for effect—but that was merely envy and spite. No one could be as desirable as Nick without inspiring a few snide remarks.

The truth was that he'd received those scars years ago, the only time he'd ever been bested. They'd been put on him to mar him, a sign of contempt for his upstart arrogance: the woman who gave them to him hadn't considered him worth killing.

But he'd learned from them. He'd learned never to be beaten again; learned to make sure that all his contests were unequal, in his favor. He'd learned to wait until he was in control of what happened. Common sense.

Members of his crew later admitted that they'd never seen his scars go as dark as when he spotted Morn Hyland. And her pale beauty ached toward him instantly—passion or desperation—bringing brightness to eyes which were dull in Angus Thermopyle's company. The only surprise was that neither of them did anything about it. The electricity between them was so strong that the spectators wouldn't have been taken aback if Morn and Nick had thrown off their clothes and jumped for each other right there in the bar.

Most of the crowd had no idea what restrained them. She was a mystery, of course. But he certainly didn't have a reputation for restraint.

Nearly two weeks later, however, they did what everyone was waiting for. When Com-Mine Security broke into Mallorys and charged Angus Thermopyle with a crime serious enough to make an arrest succeed even in DelSec, Morn Hyland was suddenly at Nick's side. And just as suddenly they were gone. Lust and common sense. Their charged flesh drew them together; and she got away from Angus at just the right moment. They left to become the kind of story drunks and dreamers told each other early in the Station's standard morning, when Mallorys was quiet and the thin alloy walls seemed safe against the hard vacuum of space and the luring madness of the gap.

The last anyone heard, Angus was rotting as predicted under a life sentence in the Station lockup.

That, of course, was not the real story.

CHAPTER 2

Some of the people who lurked in the dim light knew better. They were the ones in the corners who drank less than they appeared to, smoked less, talked less. Pushing their mugs around in the condensation which oozed off the plastic because the air processing in DelSec was never as good as it should be and nobody could sit in Mallorys without sweating, these men knew how to listen, how to ask questions, how to interpret what they saw—and when to go somewhere else for information.

Most of them were a bit older, a bit less self-absorbed; perhaps a bit more profound in their cynicism. If they were pilots, they were here because this was the life they could afford and understand, not because drink or drugs, incompetence or misjudgment, had cost them their careers. If they were miners who couldn't get or no longer wanted work, they were here to stay near the taste and dreams of prospecting, the vision of a strike so vast and pure that it was better than being rich. If they were born or naturalized inhabitants of the Station, they were here to keep company with the clientele for their particular goods or services—or perhaps to keep tabs on the market for the whispers and hints they purveyed.

Such people looked at what they saw with more discerning eyes.

When Morn Hyland and Angus Thermopyle came into Mallorys, the men in the corners noticed the way her whole body seemed to twist away even when she sat close beside him. They heard the dull, almost lifeless sound of her voice when she spoke—a tone of suppression unexpected from someone who had presumably spent weeks or months away from people and drink. And they observed that he kept one hand constantly fisted in the pocket of his grease-stained shipsuit.

After Angus took her out, some of these men also left—but not to follow. Instead, they went to have unassuming, apparently casual conversations with people who had access to the id files in Com-Mine Station's computers.

The story they gleaned concerned something more interesting than animal passion and common sense.

By one means or another, they learned that there was a perfectly reasonable explanation for the fact that Morn Hyland wasn't known in DelSec. She'd never been there before. During her one previous layover on Com-Mine, she'd stayed in AlSec.

She'd come out from Earth on one of the really wealthy independent oreliners, a family operation so successful that she and all her relatives did everything first class because they could afford it. Crossing the gap, the Hylands had docked at Com-Mine Station, not to pick up company ore for the orbiting smelters around Earth, but to buy supplies: they were headed for the belt themselves. And since they weren't experienced miners and had never been out to the belt before, there could only be one explanation for what they were doing. Somewhere they had bought or stolen the location of an asteroid rich enough to tempt them away from their usual runs. They had caught the dream themselves and were on their way to test it against the bitter rock of the belt.

A common tale, as far as it went. Back on Earth, civilization and political power required ore. Without the resources which stations like Com-Mine supplied, no government could maintain itself in office. By some standards, the United Mining Companies, Com-Mine's corporate founder, was the only effective government in human space. As a natural consequence, every city or station of any size spawned at least one earnest, spurious, or reprobate dealer in belt charts, the treasure maps of space. Men and women with some kind of hunger in their bellies were forever buying "accurate," "secret" charts and then risking everything to cross the gap and go prospecting.

But not a successful outfit like the Hyland family. If they left a profitable ore-transportation business and converted their liner for mining, two things were certain.

They had a chart.

The chart was good.

AlSec must have been on fire with that kind of news. Otherwise DelSec would never have heard about it. Specifically, Angus would never have heard about it. As a general rule, the snobs, corporate barons, government officials, intellectuals, and high-class illegals who frequented AlSec didn't share information with the denizens of Delta Sector. And Angus Thermopyle had probably never been in AlSec in his life.

Human nature being what it was, greed and a casual indifference to scruple would have inspired any number of mine jumpers or pirates to follow the Hyland ship, *Starmaster,* when she left Com-Mine Station. But jumpers and pirates had harried Com-Mine's legitimate prospectors and liners for so long—and the battles which took place as outgoing ships fought to keep from being followed had become so fierce—that now the Station itself as a matter of policy fired on any ship which tried to pursue any other ship out of dock. To all appearances, the Hylands got away safely.

Appearances must have deceived them, however. Or else they were simply outsmarted. They had no experience with the belt, or mining, or jumpers, or pirates. And Angus Thermopyle had become as rich as the stars without ever doing a lick of honest work—and without ever having to share his wealth with any partners, backers, or crew. The Hyland ship never came back.

But Morn Hyland came back.

She came back with Angus. With a dull, almost lifeless tone to her voice, and an air of being repulsed by his physical closeness.

And he kept one fist knotted like a threat in the pocket of his shipsuit.

The men who observed these things had no other way to account for them, so they jumped to the one conclusion which made sense to them; a conclusion which suited both Angus' reputation and their own cynicism.

Without any viable external evidence, they chose to believe that he'd given her a zone implant. He had the control in his pocket.

Zone implants were illegal, of course. They were so illegal that unauthorized use carried the death penalty. But—also of course—mere questions of legality didn't stop people who worked the belt from having them on hand for emergencies.

In essence, a zone implant was a radio electrode which could be slipped between one of the skull sutures and installed in the brain, where its emissions were remarkably effective. It had been invented by a doctor trying to control grand mal epileptic seizures: its emissions blanked out the neural storm of the seizure. People thought that was where the name "zone" came from: an active implant gave an epileptic the look of being "completely zoned." But in fact medical research had quickly discovered that a variety of results could be obtained by varying the implant's emissions—by tuning the implant to different zones of the brain. Violent insanities could be tamed. Manic behaviors could be moderated. Catatonia could be relieved—or induced. Recalcitrance could be turned into cooperation. Pain could be reinterpreted as pleasure.

Volition could be suppressed. Without interrupting consciousness or coordination.

Given a broad-spectrum zone implant, which employed several electrodes, and an unscrupulous control operator, independent human beings could be transformed into intelligent, effective, and loyal slaves. Even the more common, narrower-spectrum implants could achieve comparable results by turning people into physical puppets, or by applying intense neural punishments and rewards.

Unauthorized use of a zone implant carried the death penalty automatically, inevitably; without appeal.

But despite the law—and the possibilities of abuse—even otherwise reputable miners and pilots, orehaulers and -handlers, considered zone implants necessary medical equipment.

The reason was simple. Medical science had developed ways for complete idiots to diagnose and treat complex diseases; ways for lost or vision-struck belt pilots to repair the damage done to their bodies by faulty or inadequate equipment; ways for crushed limbs and even crushed organs to be prosthetically restored. Unfortunately, however, no amount of research had discovered a cure for gap-sickness, that strange breakdown of the mind which took perhaps one out of every hundred people who crossed the dimensional gap and reduced him or her to a psychotic killer or a null-wave transmitter, a raving bulimic or a gleeful self-flagellant, a pedophiliac or a pill-junkie. Apparently, one out of every hundred people had some kind of undetectable vulnerability in the tissue of the brain; and when that vulnerability was translated across light-years of space through the imponderable physics of the gap, something happened to it. Otherwise healthy individuals lost command of their lives in invariably startling, often grotesque, and sometimes murderous fashions.

There was no cure for gap-sickness. But there was a way to cope with it.

The zone implant.

Ships and prospecting and mining operations were too fragile: every individual's life depended on everybody else. For that reason, perfectly sane and law-abiding people considered it an unacceptable risk to cross the gap or ride dark space without access to zone implants. Just in case the person standing right over there suddenly picked up a hose and started to spray mineral acid in all directions.

"Authorized use" of a zone implant occurred when the whole crew of a ship or the entire population of a mining camp testified that they would all have died if they hadn't used the implant to control a case of gap-sickness—and when the person with the implant confirmed that he or she hadn't been deprived of volition in any other situations.

The UMC Police enforced the principle of "authorized use" with almost gleeful impartiality.

In part for that reason, actual, proven cases of abuse were rare. But there were always stories. So-and-so hit a rich strike on an asteroid so far away that it was off the charts, so far away that he and his crew didn't have enough provisions to stay and mine it—a problem he solved by giving everyone else zone implants and making them work without food or water or sleep until they died. Such-and-such was prospecting alone and contrived to smash his leg with his ship's cargo boom; in pain and delirious, he neglected normal medical treatment and instead supplied himself with a zone implant in order to change the pain into pleasure—with the result that he became so happy he lost his mind and bled to death.

What the men in the bars and sleeps of DelSec talked about most often, however, was women. Women were rare on mining stations. Single women were even rarer. And available women were so rare that they were prohibitively expensive; which meant that most of them lived in AlSec. Men with nothing better to do rarely thought about anything else. Gorgeous women. Astonishing women. Women with zone implants, who did everything a drink-fuddled or cynical mind could imagine. Because they didn't have any choice, no matter how much they may have hated what was happening to them.

Women like Morn Hyland.

So what must have happened was that Angus Thermopyle found a way to follow the Hyland ship when it left Com-Mine Station.

After all, who knew how much sophisticated tracking equipment he had hidden away aboard his scruffy, rattletrap freighter? With all the mines he was said to have jumped, all the ore he was believed to have pirated, all the ships he was reputed to have wrecked, his financial resources must have been enormous. He could surely afford things over which even a successful swashbuckler like Nick Succorso could only drool. Obviously, he wasn't spending the money on himself. Anybody who had to sit near him in Mallorys would have sworn he hadn't changed his shipsuit since the invention of the gap drive. He never bought expensive drinks—or more than a few cheap ones. And he absolutely never bought expensive women.

As for his ship, which he called by the odd, inapt name, *Bright Beauty,* no one ever saw inside her; but her exterior plate and ports and antennae and scanners looked like they had been driven through a meteor shower and then left to corrode. In fact, the only discernible care he took of her—the only hint he gave that he had any interest in her at all—was to keep her name freshly painted in crisp black letters on either side of her command module.

What was he doing with all that money?

What else? He must be investing it in his "business," using it to buy the kind of vacuum sniffers and particle sifters and doppler sensors that most pilots who frequented Com-Mine Station only knew about by rumor; the kind of equipment which would allow him to follow the Hyland ship without making either her or the Station itself suspicious.

There were still questions unanswered. Everyone knew that a ship the size of *Bright Beauty* needed at least two people and preferably six to run her. Assuming that Morn Hyland worked for him on his return, Angus must still have had a crew of some kind when he left on *Starmaster*'s trail. Who was it? Presumably, it must have been someone who had managed to get on and off Com-Mine Station without id processing, since *Bright Beauty* had no crew of record in the computer. So what happened to him? Or them?

What happened to the Hyland ship and all the rest of her people?

No one knew. But Angus Thermopyle must have followed them to their strike. He must have jumped them somehow—wrecked the ship, marooned or murdered the family. And spared Morn because under the persuasion of the zone implant she was as desirable as any vision.

Because—so speculation ran—he hated her.

It was nothing personal, of course. He hated everything. He hated everybody. The people who watched for such things could smell it on him. His life was a stew of hate, destructive and unpredictable. Now his hate was fixed on her, and he desired the thing he hated. He wanted her to be what only a zone implant could make her.

Beautiful and revolted. Capable of any degradation his filthy appetites could conceive—and able to be hurt by it.

The few men in Mallorys who realized what they considered the truth about her were sickened by it. Being of various moral characters themselves, some of them probably considered it evil. The rest probably considered it evil that the control to her implant was in Angus Thermopyle's pocket.

On this subject, Nick Succorso kept his opinion to himself. Perhaps his attraction to Morn was so strong that he didn't think about anything else.

Despite his attraction, however, and his reputation for success, he was probably restrained from immediate action by the prospect of what Angus might do if he were challenged. To Morn Hyland, of course. But also to whoever challenged him. He had a history of getting rid of his enemies. So instead of leaping to her rescue, Nick waited and plotted. He may have been a criminal or a rogue hero, an operative or a mercenary; but he certainly wasn't stupid. And he had no taste at all for defeat.

What he wanted—so the discerning cynics assumed—was to have Angus arrested by Security with the control to Morn's zone implant in his pocket. Angus would get the death penalty; the implant would be removed; and then Morn Hyland would be free to give Nick Succorso the only reward he could possibly want.

Herself.

The hard part was to arrange for Angus to be arrested. He

wasn't an easy victim. Piracy, treachery, and murder were what he did best.

Nevertheless Nick arranged it.

Once again, the only explanations available were purely speculative. In the Station lockup, Angus wasn't talking to anybody. And Nick Succorso and his crew were gone, taking Morn Hyland with them. But here speculation was on fairly solid ground. Knowing Nick, it was possible to guess with considerable confidence what he would do.

His background was vague. His id files managed to look both perfectly legitimate and plainly spurious, revealing nothing. All most people knew was that one day he docked his pretty frigate, *Captain's Fancy,* in Com-Mine Station, passed inspection, led his crew into DelSec, selected Mallorys Bar & Sleep apparently at random, and became a regular whenever he was on station. Only the men in the corners, the men who pried below the surface, heard how he had passed inspection.

Being neither asleep nor blind, the Station inspectors had noticed almost immediately that *Captain's Fancy* had a hole the size of a gaming table in her side.

You've been hit, they said. That looks like matter cannon fire.

It is, he replied.

Why were you being shot at?

I wasn't.

No? The inspectors suggested intense skepticism.

No. I was trying to get inside one of those awkward asteroids— too small for heavy equipment, too big to be chewed up by hand-cutters. So I decided to try blasting it apart. Somehow, the matter beam hit a glazed surface and reflected back. Nick grinned amiably. I shot myself.

That doesn't sound very plausible, Captain Succorso. Hand over your computer's datacore, and we'll verify your story.

No, he said again. Now his grin didn't look so amiable. I'm not required to let you look at my datacore unless you have evidence of a crime. That's the law. Has there been a crime?

In the end, Nick passed. The ship that shot him must have been burned out of space in return, so it was never able to report that a crime had been committed.

Smiling to make DelSec's women's hearts flutter, basking in the devotion of his crew, and spending money as if he had a UMC credit line, he settled into Mallorys and concentrated on enjoying himself while *Captain's Fancy* was repaired. He seemed to have a talent for enjoying himself, and his good humor—like his unmistakable virility—was infectious. Only people who watched the scars under his eyes could tell that he was engaged in anything more serious than a continuous carouse. And in Mallorys that "anything" could be only one thing: he was listening, sifting, sorting, evaluating; making contact with sources of information.

Whenever he left Com-Mine Station, he left suddenly. And when he came back, he celebrated.

By some coincidence, unfamiliar ships had a tendency to go "overdue" while he was away.

Even a null-wave transmitter could have predicted that everything inside Nick would leap up at the sight of Morn Hyland. If he was a pirate, he was the glamorous kind, the kind who slashed and burned his way to virtue in romantic videos. And she was beautiful and pathetic—a maiden in distress if ever there was one, abused and helpless. Not to mention the fact that she belonged to someone else, a pirate rumored to be even more successful than Nick Succorso himself. But only the people who didn't know any better were surprised that he didn't try to rescue her right away. The men in the corners could guess what he would do.

He wouldn't try to steal her directly. He was too smart for that. In other words, he had too much respect for Angus Thermopyle's defenses. And Angus kept his vulnerabilities—as well as his debaucheries—private by sealing them safely aboard *Bright Beauty*. Station Security itself would have come to his assistance if Nick had tried to get past his alarms.

No, Nick would sit and listen, watching Morn Hyland until his scars turned black and waiting for his chance; waiting for Angus Thermopyle to make a move.

He wanted to see that move coming and know what it would be. He wanted to do what Security had never been able to do—penetrate Angus' secrecy. And when he knew what Angus' move would be, he would follow it so that he could betray it. The moment in which Angus was arrested might be Nick's only realistic opportunity to carry Morn away.

He wanted her.

He also wanted to prove himself against Angus Thermopyle.

If he had other reasons, he never gave a hint of them to DelSec.

As it happened, his chance came sooner than he may have expected. Maybe Angus felt cocky with Morn beside him and wanted to show off. Or maybe he was getting greedy—if in fact he could conceivably be any greedier than he was already. Or maybe the bait was just too attractive to be ignored. Whatever the reason, he made his move scarcely two weeks after he first brought Morn into Mallorys.

The incoming supply ship from Earth—arriving several weeks early for some reason—was in trouble. Every receiver in or around the Station picked up the distress call before it went dead. Apparently one of the crew had been taken by gap-sickness. As the ship reentered normal space, this unfortunate individual had become entranced by the idea of installing a crowbar in the memory bank of the navigational computer. By the time his shipmates got him under control, the ship could no longer steer and had no idea where she was. The fact that the distress call went dead seemed to imply that the damage to the computer—perhaps a fire—had spread to the communication gear.

In other words, a full standard year's worth of food, equipment, and medicine was floating out there somewhere against the background of the stars, ripe to be rescued, salvaged, or gutted.

Of course, as soon as the emergency was understood, Com-Mine Center slapped a curfew onto the docks, forbidding any ship to leave until she could be sworn in as part of the official search; until Security personnel could be put aboard to watch the actions of the crew. That was standard procedure. And it was generally respected, even by pirates and jumpers. Ships that shared in the search also shared in the reward, regardless of which vessel actually performed the rescue, while ships that violated curfew, refused to cooperate, or went off on their own became targets by law and could be fired on with impunity.

This time, only *Bright Beauty* and *Captain's Fancy* took that chance. Somehow, both Angus Thermopyle and Nick Succorso managed to uncouple from their berths seconds before the injunction of the curfew, thus preserving at least the illusion of authorized departure.

Center wasn't impressed by illusions, however. Commands to return and redock were broadcast: warning shots were fired.

With contemptuous ease, *Captain's Fancy* winked off the scanners of the Station.

Nick Succorso disappeared by performing a delicate maneuver called a "blink crossing." No one in Mallorys doubted his ability to do this. In essence, he engaged his gap drive—and then disengaged it a fraction of a second later, thereby forcing his ship to "blink" past fifty or a hundred thousand kilometers. It was risky: there was always the chance that dimensional stress would tear the ship apart, or that he would come out of the gap in a gravity well he couldn't escape. But it worked. He got away.

From the look of her, *Bright Beauty* would never have withstood that much pressure. In any case, she had no gap drive. Angus Thermopyle took a completely different approach. As soon as the first warning shots were fired, he started transmitting a distress call of his own.

Every receiver in or around the Station picked that one up too. *There's a short somewhere. Smoke. Controls are locked—I can't navigate. Don't shoot. I'm trying to come around.*

No one believed him, of course. But Center couldn't afford to ignore the possibility that he might be telling the truth. That idea had to be considered, at least for a few seconds. And during those few seconds Angus cut in thrust boosters no one knew he had. No one thought he had them because no one believed *Bright Beauty* could survive that kind of acceleration.

Like Nick, he got away.

After that, there were no more answers for a while. The people who were following the story could speculate, but for two days they had nothing to base their speculations on.

Then *Bright Beauty* came limping back. Her sides were scarred with matter cannon fire, and her thrust drive stuttered badly. Nevertheless she passed inspection. Angus Thermopyle faced down a board of inquiry. After a few hours, he brought Morn Hyland back to Mallorys. Neither of them gave anything away.

*Captain's Fancy* coasted into dock later the same day. She also had been hurt, but Nick Succorso didn't seem to care. He talked her past inspection. He laughed circles around a board of inquiry. He and his crew also returned to Mallorys free and eager, ready to enjoy themselves.

The official search was still going on. So far, no trace of the supply ship had been found. After this much time, there was little chance that any trace would ever be found.

But that night Station Security broke into Mallorys to arrest Angus.

They had evidence that a crime had been committed. So they said. That gave them the right to board *Bright Beauty* without permission and take the ship's datacore. The datacore enabled them to find her secret holds. And in the secret holds were food, equipment, and medicine which could only have come from the missing supply ship.

Arrests in DelSec were few. The people who frequented places like Mallorys Bar & Sleep were prone to resent the intrusion of overt law and order into their lives. Even in groups, Security couldn't always pass through DelSec without harassment.

But a supply ship had been robbed—presumably gutted. Com-Mine Station needed those supplies to live. DelSec needed those supplies. Every man and woman in Mallorys would have suffered for this particular crime. And every one of them disliked or feared or even hated Angus Thermopyle.

At first, the arrest didn't go smoothly. Before Angus was taken, he and Morn Hyland began to scuffle: he was apparently trying to hold her back. Nevertheless she managed to break away just as Security closed on him. At once, the crowd opened for her, pried apart by Nick Succorso's crew. And then she and Nick were gone; they disappeared as effectively as a blink crossing.

*Captain's Fancy* was allowed to slip out of dock unmolested; but that wasn't hard to explain. Nick must have done a certain amount of bargaining with Security before he handed over his evidence against Angus. Obviously, his right to leave was part of the bargain.

So the fair maiden was rescued. The swashbuckling pirate bore her away with all her beauty. For weeks, the sots and relics in Mallorys could hardly talk about anything except what the maiden and the pirate were doing with each other. People who were accessible to romantic emotions contemplated what had happened with a lump in their throats. And even the cynics sitting in the corners were gratified by the outcome. Nick Succorso had done exactly what they expected of him.

There were only two flaws in this story.

One was that the supply ship from Earth arrived on schedule. It hadn't had any trouble along the way. And it reported that there hadn't been any other ship.

The other was that the control to Morn Hyland's zone implant was never found. Angus Thermopyle didn't have it on him when he was arrested. That was why he was rotting in lockup instead of facing execution.

The first matter was easily explained. Nick Succorso must have arranged the whole thing—faked the distress call, stolen Station supplies himself, planted them on *Bright Beauty*. That was the kind of thing he did. It made the people in Mallorys admire him even more.

The second issue was more disconcerting, however. It didn't make sense. Angus could not have gotten rid of the control earlier: if he had done that, she would have been able to escape him—or, more likely, to butcher him with her bare hands for the things he had done to her. And yet he must have gotten rid of it earlier. Otherwise he would have been caught with it.

The only other explanation was less satisfying. After all, the zone implant and its control were hypothetical, not proven. Perhaps they had never existed.

But in that case the entire sequence of events degenerated into incomprehensibility. Why did she stay with him, if he had no power over her? And if his power was of some other kind, why did he give it up? What warned him that he was in danger?

No one knew the answers. However, the people who asked them were only interested out of curiosity. The main thrust of the action was clear enough. Details that didn't make sense could eventually be forgotten.

The crowd at Mallorys would have found the real story much harder to live with.

CHAPTER 3

There were parts of the story that would always remain obscure, unless Angus Thermopyle explained them; and he refused.

By the end of his trial, *Bright Beauty* didn't have any secrets left. Despite her pretense of being a prospector's ship, she was indeed equipped with sophisticated particle sifters and doppler sensors, tools that no legitimate prospector would ever need. She was too heavily shielded, too heavily armed. Under boost, her thrust drive could have shifted the orbit of a planetoid. She had cargo holds hidden in places the Station inspectors never imagined. And she had so many relays and servos, compensations and overrides, that it was actually possible for one man to run her alone—although the experts who examined her agreed it would be suicide for any individual to take on that kind of complex strain for more than a few hours at a time.

In addition, the datacore revealed the extent of Angus' "wealth."

To the surprise of his prosecutors, his resources turned out to be trivial; almost nonexistent. Regardless of his reputation, he was operating only a few steps ahead of his expenses.

That unexpected detail didn't help him, of course. He hadn't been arrested for his "wealth." And in other ways the exposure of his secrets was sufficiently damning. Enough evidence was found to convict him of several acts of piracy—although everyone in Security agreed that the evidence was disappointing, since it wasn't adequate to procure the death penalty. Certainly it wasn't adequate to explain the more tantalizing aspects of Morn's story.

Confronted with this inadequacy—which presumably gave him the opportunity to cast his actions in the most favorable possible light—Angus surprised his prosecutors further by refusing to defend himself, testify on his own behalf. Indeed, he refused to answer any questions at all. With a zone implant, of course, he could have been inspired to talk; but the law—and the UMCP—refused to consider confession an "authorized use." Consequently, Com-Mine Security never found out where or how *Bright Beauty* had been outfitted, or how she'd been damaged. No explanation was obtained for the fact that his reputation so far exceeded the evidence against him. He was unwilling either to account for or to defend the presence of stolen Station food, equipment, and medicine aboard his ship. And no new illumination was shed on his strange relationship with Morn Hyland. In the first weeks of his incarceration, he opened his mouth only when he wanted to complain about the food or the facilities or the treatment in the Station lockup.

And when he was informed that *Bright Beauty* was being sent to the Station shipyard to be dismantled for spare parts. Then he pounded on the walls of his cell and started to howl with such fury that eventually he had to be sedated.

No one knew what had warned him when the Hyland ship had come into Com-Mine Station—or how hard he had tried to get away from her.

Probably he would have been unable to explain that warning. It was a matter of instinct. He had good instincts, and they started to burn as he watched the sleek oreliner nudge its way into dock.

It looked like a prize, the kind of treasure ship *Bright Beauty* could peel apart weld by weld, exposing to theft or destruction the things that made other people think they were superior beings: the money, the possessions, the luck. He had tackled ships like that in the past, had tackled them often, tracking them to their destinations, learning their secrets, then blasting them open in the black void, leaving them ruined, lost forever—had tackled them and raged to himself fiercely as he did so, destroying what other men would have captured as riches because his need for money had limits while his desire to see what matter cannon fire could do was immense. Alone in his ship, or wandering around DelSec, or sitting in Mallorys— Angus Thermopyle was always alone, even when he happened to find some stow- or castaway piece of human garbage to crew for him—he relived the ships he had tackled and hated them.

But not this time.

This time, his instincts burned—and he always trusted his instincts.

As far as he knew, he had no particular reason to be wary. His crimes left little evidence behind; there was no better place than deep space to hide the remains of his plundering. Only his datacore could damage him, and he had long ago taken steps to alleviate that danger—steps which no one would detect because they were theoretically impossible. But because he was a hunter, he had also been hunted. He had the intuitions of prey.

So he did something that would never have occurred to anyone else on or around Com-Mine Station: he turned his field-mining probes toward the Hyland ship.

One of those probes was designed to measure the nuclear weight of thin cross sections of solid rock. It informed him that *Starmaster*'s hull was formed of an alloy he'd only heard about, never seen—an alloy so heavy it could shed matter cannon fire the way steel shed water.

An alloy so expensive no oreliner could afford it. There were no haulers or handlers in space rich enough to afford it.

When he saw the readings, Angus Thermopyle fled.

He didn't take the time to buy supplies. He didn't try to find out what the station scuttlebutt concerning the Hyland ship was. He didn't even bother to repaint *Bright Beauty*'s name—something he always did before risking the malign vagaries of space. A ship as rich as *Starmaster* would have friends, muscle. Escorts? Fighters hanging off station to watch for trouble? He took that into account, but it didn't stop him. Sealing his hatches, he called up Station Center, filed a purely fictitious destination report, and received formal permission to undock. Then, because his instincts were still on fire, he meticulously followed the departure trajectory he was assigned. Cursing like a slavey all the way, he left Com-Mine along a route that would attract as little attention as possible. And he didn't risk cutting in boost and shifting his course toward the belt until he was absolutely alone at least fifty thousand kilometers past the known range of any scan from the vicinity of Station.

He was hoping that the belt was far enough away to hide him. The Station had been built at a considerable distance to avoid the meteor storms and other debris which always accompanied asteroid belts through space, the residue of planets that time and gravity had reduced to rubble.

By the time he changed course, the exertion of manning the

whole ship himself had begun to make his hands shake and his eyes fill with sweat. He had too many instruments to read, too many systems to monitor, too much data to absorb. And his computer couldn't help him. It had extravagant fail-safes: the very mechanisms which enabled him to run *Bright Beauty* alone would shut the ship down in alarm if he gave the computer control of them. Nevertheless he kept going. His instincts had warned him, and he always obeyed them.

Angus Thermopyle was a pirate and a mine jumper. He hated everybody, and there was enough old blood on his hands to convict a whole prison full of illegals. He was alone now because the decrepit drunk he'd hired to crew for him had made the mistake of asking the wrong question at the wrong time; so he'd flattened the man's head with a spanner and left the body in one of the thruster tubes to be ashed the next time the drive was engaged. He may not have been rich, but he was probably everything else the people in Mallorys believed him to be.

He was also a coward.

So he ran from the Hyland ship under as much g as his body could stand and remain conscious. The muscles of his shoulders began to twitch, and he couldn't keep the sweat out of his eyes; but he kept running. When he knew that he had pushed himself too far, he didn't stop: instead, he started pumping drugs into his veins, stim to keep him awake, cat to keep him steady.

He was afraid, and he ran.

Before he was close enough to the belt to begin deceleration, he had been driving under heavy g for half a standard day. Now the drugs were giving him psychotic episodes with increasing regularity, and he no longer knew clearly what he was doing. However, he was familiar with those drugs; before starting them, he'd understood what they would do to him. So he'd taken the precaution of locking *Bright Beauty*'s course. When he was finally forced to surrender control of his ship's systems to her command computer, the course-lock and her fail-safes managed the hard braking for him. As a result, he arrived without crashing—and without pulling his ship away into madness—at a part of the belt which everyone knew had been mined out years ago; a long stretch of sailing rock where other ships were unlikely to come.

There he picked a particularly dead asteroid, parked *Bright Beauty* in a mining crater, shut down everything except life-support, and went to sleep in his g-seat, catted out of his mind.

If the Hyland ship could find him there, then he was lost anyway. He had never really had a chance to escape.

He still had no reason to believe the people on that ship even knew he existed.

Hours later, he awoke screaming because there were skinworms all over him, crawling, gnawing, starting to burrow in—

The sensation was terrible. It was also normal; a predictable consequence of the drugs. However, for him so much of what was terrible was also familiar that he knew exactly what to do. Although he couldn't swallow the bright terror rising in his throat or unknot the red pain closing around his heart, his hands were almost steady as he injected more drugs into his veins—analgesics to flush the now-poisonous stimulants and cataleptics away, antihistamines and steroids to soften his body's reactions. As soon as these new drugs took hold, he slept again.

The next time he awakened, he had trouble breathing because the air in *Bright Beauty* was going bad. He'd left Com-Mine Station without supplies. That meant he now had only a little water, less food—and no clean pads for the scrubbers which were supposed to keep his air breathable. Checking the computer's maintenance log, he confirmed that his present pads were long overdue for a change.

This development made him rage as if he were on the verge of a breakdown. But that, too, was normal. He still knew exactly what to do. Risking anoxia because he didn't have the strength to put on an EVA suit, he shut down circulation and took the pads out of the scrubbers. While his head throbbed with $CO_2$ overload and his vision blurred in and out of focus, he used half his water to make a chemical bath for the pads. He left the pads in the bath as long as he could—until he was close to unconsciousness. Then he refitted them in the scrubbers and restarted the circulation.

Unfortunately, his problems were just beginning.

He was probably safe where he was; but he couldn't stay there. His food would last for only two or three more days. He could reuse all his water—but only if he had his purifiers serviced. And the superficial cleaning he'd given the pads might not hold up even that long. He had only two choices.

Return to Com-Mine Station.

Or find some other source of supply.

He never considered returning to the Station. He wasn't deterred by the prospect of humiliation. If anyone ever found out that he'd panicked and run, only to return limping because he'd run out of food, water, and air, he would be sneered at everywhere in DelSec; but he could live with that. The world had been sneering at him from the first. He took revenge when he got the chance. However, there was still the Hyland ship—

That ship was to blame, of course. She'd scared him, and he hated everything that scared him. As he lifted *Bright Beauty* out of the mining crater and eased back from the belt to give his scanning equipment range, he began to plot ways to make *Starmaster* pay for what was happening to him.

Ways to wreck a ship with *that* hull? The bare concept was nonsense—and Angus Thermopyle wasn't prone to nonsense.

Nevertheless thinking about it helped him do what he had to. In a state of cold rage which served as calm, he spent the next two days searching the belt with his sniffers and sifters, prospecting not for ore but for miners.

Toward the end of that time, he came close to panic again. The pads were starting to give out; his brain was being squeezed in a vise of bad air. His tongue was thick from drinking bad water, and he was urgently hungry. Still his cold, black rage kept him going. And a judicious application of drugs kept him steady.

At last he found what he needed—a mine on a craggy and pockmarked asteroid with a look of depletion about it, as if it had already had all its riches cut out. Yet the people working there had a ship. It stood on its struts a short distance from their camp, which was in turn a short distance from the hole they'd cut into the asteroid. The ship was cold: it had been shut down a considerable time ago, when the miners had settled in to work this hunk of rock.

Under other circumstances, Angus Thermopyle would have ignored those miners. He could tell their whole story with a glance at their ship, their camp, and his field-mining probes. This asteroid had once been rich, but it had in fact already been mined; played out. The people on it now—probably a family, people who had to spend long periods of time on ships or in mines tended to do things by families—were essentially scavengers. Too timid or defeated or poor to go prospecting for an original strike, they sweated their bare survival out of the rock by gleaning what little had been missed by previous miners. A pirate or jumper wouldn't waste his time on them.

On the other hand, they had food and fresh water and scrubber pads. Angus was having trouble keeping his anger and distress from choking him, and he didn't hesitate. He went in hard.

The miners saw him coming. His board picked up shouts of

warning and protest, appeal and outrage: he ignored them. As he approached, he used torpedoes to collapse the mouth of the mine, blocking it with dead rock. Then he set *Bright Beauty* straight down on the camp so that his braking blast incinerated the habitation domes, charred the suited figures outside.

The radio shouts died in a gabble of static. Got you, you bastards. The camp had been large enough to support perhaps twenty people. With luck, he'd killed them all. He didn't want any witnesses.

A quick scan for life readings, distress calls, suit-to-suit communications. None. Good. That left him with a clear path to the other ship. As soon as he put on a suit himself, he could go over there and get everything he needed. Then he would be able to hide out in the belt as long as necessary. Until he got a chance to repay some of his fear.

He was on his way to the EVA locker when *Bright Beauty*'s Klaxons went off like several dozen screams of pain.

The asteroid's tiny gravity didn't hold him back: with a powerful kick, he sent himself diving for the command module. One hand caught the back of his g-seat; the other slapped instructions at the computer, demanding an explanation. He was already in the seat, strapped down, and keying thrust for takeoff by the time the computer told him what was going on.

His sifters and sniffers and sensors had detected the approach of another ship. And not just any other ship: a ship the same size and configuration as *Starmaster*.

In fact, it was *Starmaster*. His probes weren't likely to be mistaken about that alloy. He'd programmed the computer to watch for her. And to make enough noise to wake him from his grave if it spotted her.

She was coming at him fast.

How the fucking hell did she *get* here? How did she *find* me?

No time for that. Coming fast. But not fast enough to catch him. *Bright Beauty* was bound to be more agile than any oreliner, no matter how much cash that bitch cost. And this was the belt, where agility was worth more than matter cannon fire. He was terrified— but he also knew what he could do. What his ship could do. Let that fornicating hunk of money try to chase him and see what happened.

The only problem was that he didn't have enough food. Or water. Or air.

No time for that either. Survival was the highest priority Angus Thermopyle understood: it took precedence over everything. And he was sure from the core of his bloated belly to the sweat rolling down his jowls that the Hyland ship didn't intend him to survive. As if he really were calm, he hit thrust and began lift-off. At the same time, he primed his cannon, diverting precious boost to build up charge. And he made sure his communications board was clear, set to receive everything and transmit nothing.

*Starmaster* was still a considerable distance away, but her first transmission reached him before he was a hundred meters off the asteroid.

"Set down." The voice sounded crisp and commanding above the hull-roar of thrust. "*Bright Beauty,* you are ordered to set down."

Despite the intensity of his concentration on his instruments and controls, Angus was able to mutter a few obscenities under his breath.

"Angus Thermopyle, you are ordered to set down." The voice was sure of itself. "This is Captain Davies Hyland, commanding officer, United Mining Companies Police destroyer *Starmaster.* You have committed murder. If you do not set down to be boarded, you will be fired upon."

UMCP. That got his attention. For a second, he actually

stopped swearing and took his hands off his console. The cops. It made sense; so much sense that he should have figured it out earlier. Who else was there anywhere who could pool enough money to hull an entire ship with that alloy? Who else thought they owned the fucking universe? No one. Only the United Mining Companies—and their private cops, the muscle which enforced or invented the law that kept Earth and its huge appetites fed.

And this was why they were here: to hunt the pirates and jumpers and scavengers who fed off all the mining operations in vast space. In just a few seconds, they would be close enough to ash him.

"Message repeats," the radio announced, stupidly unafraid. "Angus Thermopyle, you are ordered to set down. This is Captain Davies Hyland, commanding officer, United Mining—"

"No," Angus coughed in desperation. With one heavy finger he stabbed at his console, cut off reception. At once, the noise of his thrusters through the hull seemed to get louder, more frantic. "I don't care if you come from fucking *God*. You can't have my *ship*."

Holding his breath against the stress, he wrenched *Bright Beauty* around scarcely two hundred meters off the asteroid and slammed on full boost, piling up more g than he ought to be able to stand in order to put the asteroid between him and *Starmaster*. Then he drove away toward the heart of the belt.

He didn't cut thrust, reduce acceleration, until the simple weight of his body under so much g pushed him to the edge of blackout.

Klaxons howled at him, proximity sensors squalling with overload. Light-headed in physical relief as g eased—relief that didn't touch his essential terror—Angus skimmed past a small meteor, then deflected *Bright Beauty* between two larger rocks. At the same time, he rigged his ship for battle.

Under normal operating conditions, she required two people to run her. In combat situations, she could have used six. But Angus Thermopyle handled everything himself.

He made no effort to turn his cannon on the UMCP ship. Instead, as fast as his targeting computer could track, he started blazing away at every meteor and asteroid in range, filling the space behind him with chunks of all sizes caroming in all directions; covering his tail with debris. He wasn't trying to lure *Starmaster* into a crash; not yet: she was still too far away to be threatened by a little rubble. But she was closing fast—and a destroyer as expensive as she was probably had artillery which would make his cannon look like popguns. He was doing his best to confuse her targ.

It worked for a while. Out of the black, light came in bright flares, matter fire hitting rock; the rock went incandescent as it burst into its component particles; static sizzled across *Bright Beauty*'s scan; light collapsed to black again. Angus rode a meson torrent deeper into the belt and snatched his ship past obstacles that could have crushed her, and went on firing himself, madly throwing up scree like a screen against *Starmaster*'s guns.

But the destroyer learned fast. She turned his own tactics against him. There was a lull in the fire—fifteen seconds, twenty, twenty-five—during which no attempt was made to hit him. Then a dead stone lump the size of a small space station hardly a thousand kilometers ahead took a shaft of incandescence through its center and broke apart so violently that chunks as big as ejection pods came at him like thunderbolts.

His proximity alarms went wild, then dead as their circuits overloaded.

In the sudden silence, Angus ducked, squirmed, twisted—and almost made it. *Bright Beauty* was agile, and he was desperate. At the last instant, however, one rock slapped her in the side and sent her tumbling like a derelict through the belt.

The next collision was gentler, just a kiss that flattened out some of the gyration. He didn't feel it. G and anoxia had stretched him too thin. He was unconscious. As far as he knew, he was still trying to scream.

CHAPTER 4

M oments later, he came back to himself. Just in time: *Bright Beauty* was plunging toward the kind of collision that would crumple her like an empty can. Hardly aware yet of what he was doing, reacting by plain instinct and fear, he punched at his console, fought the spin, got his thrusters aimed for braking. Only a few hundred meters off an asteroid almost large enough for colonization, he wrestled his ship under control.

Running on automatic pilot himself, still gasping for air and barely able to focus his eyes, he checked for damage. *Bright Beauty* had a cabin-size dent in her side; but her shields held, interior bulkheads held, preserving a fragile integrity. One part of her nose looked like it'd been hit by an impact-ram, and a number of sensors and sniffers were dead; but no structural harm had been done. She would still function. She could go someplace and get help—at the moment, he had no idea where, his brain was too fuzzy from oxygen starvation, but *some*place, it was still possible, she could do it somehow.

Entirely by accident, one of the cameras which had been scanning *Bright Beauty*'s hull gave him a glimpse of the UMCP ship.

She was coming for him, coming fast.

She had a straight shot at him. As soon as she fired, his whole life would be reduced to light and electrons.

And there was nothing he could do about it. He couldn't even play dead. That wouldn't fool her. She'd seen him brake: she knew he was alive.

The thought turned his guts to water. He didn't want to die. Almost without realizing it, he hit his distress beacon. Don't shoot, don't shoot, you fornicating filthy bastards, *don't kill me,* I surrender.

*Starmaster* came ahead as if she wanted to eviscerate him at point-blank range; as if Captain Davies Hyland wanted to see Angus Thermopyle die with his own eyes.

The terrible injustice of it made Angus burn to shoot first, to key targ and at least go out fighting, even though matter cannon fire couldn't hurt the UMCP ship. But he didn't do that. Fear was more imperative than hate. Raging like a maniac, he fed his transmitter all the gain it could handle and sent his distress call into the dark like a wail.

His cameras gave him a perfect view as *Starmaster* altered course, turned in the direction of the asteroid—and broke in half.

*Broke in half.*

A blast like that: one of the drives must have blown up. Fire and metal sprayed without a sound into the belt. Out of the center of the explosion, *Starmaster* toppled as if she were falling toward the surface of the asteroid.

Angus watched in complete astonishment as the ship crashed and died.

Instead of gutting *Starmaster,* the fire went out almost immediately. That implied— He was too stupefied to realize what it implied. On automatic again, his hands fumbled across the console, activating short-range scanners, focusing cameras. He was trying to think. He should already be dead, fried in his g-seat. The UMCP ship had a straight shot at him. But he was still alive. *Starmaster* broke in half. The fire went out almost immediately.

That implied—

Oxygen.

The fire went out because it didn't get oxygen. But the ship was full of air. Angus understood fires in space: he knew *Starmaster* should have burned longer than that. Some of her interior bulkheads must be holding. Parts of her retained structural integrity.

That, too, had significant implications. They eluded him, however. Bad air and the fundamental shock of his survival muddled his head. Ideas that should have been clear to him refused to come into focus.

Then he got it.

If parts of *Starmaster* retained integrity, then some of her people might have been protected or shielded. There might be survivors.

There were survivors. When he pulled his eyes down from the screen where his cameras reported what they could see, down to his scan displays and readouts, he discovered that his instruments registered life. Three or four people were still alive.

No, not three. Definitely four.

Still stunned by what had happened, and hardly able to breathe because *Bright Beauty*'s atmosphere had deteriorated considerably during the past few minutes, Angus struggled to think.

He never considered trying to rescue the survivors. Even with all his wits about him, he would have dismissed that idea. Those people were cops; his enemies. And he didn't bother to wonder what had happened, how *Starmaster* had died. He would probably never know the answer to that question. He would probably never care. His thoughts were more basic:

Air.

Water.

Food.

And he thought, Bastards! If he went down there, one of the survivors might shoot him. He would have to wait here until they were dead.

But he didn't know how badly they were hurt. If they were hurt at all. They might be able to outlast him. Without adequate air or water or food, he might collapse long before they did.

Caught between need and cowardice, he was paralyzed. Sucking sweat off his upper lip, he stared at *Starmaster*'s image on his screen and wrestled with his fear.

Then he thought about what had been done to him.

His heart began to swell with old rage, familiar and malign. The strength which had kept him alive so long, against such odds, came back to him. Snarling curses as fiercely as he could with the little oxygen the rank atmosphere provided, he shifted *Bright Beauty* into landing attitude and started her moving.

While he was still negotiating a touchdown, scan informed him that one set of life-signs had stopped.

Good. Only three left.

Gently he set *Bright Beauty* on her struts beside the UMCP ship. Leaving his g-seat, he bobbed like a balloon against the asteroid's gravity toward her lockers.

Once he'd donned his EVA suit and clamped the faceplate shut, he spent a minute simply breathing the sweet air from the tanks. But he couldn't afford to delay. The remaining survivors might be aware of him. They might be trying to train *Starmaster*'s guns on him right now.

He took an impact rifle with him, a miner's weapon because it could clear rockfalls and powder stone; in a pinch it could be used to buckle steel plate. He was no longer swearing: he was too scared to swear. The UMCP ship terrified him. The survivors terrified him. And EVA always terrified him. But he thought about air and revenge, and went to get them.

Cycling through the airlocks, he eased himself onto the surface of the asteroid.

Out here, the only light was the distant glitter of the starfield. Without the enhanced sensitivity of his cameras to help him, he could only see *Starmaster* as a silhouette, blacker than space. She looked huge and treacherous, riddled with secrets. Playing a beam along her sides helped put her in perspective; but that small light couldn't muffle the way his air tanks hissed in his ears, sounding so loud against the impenetrable silence of the belt that it seemed to mark him like a beacon for all his enemies. He loathed EVA because the sound of his own breathing made him feel puny and vulnerable. Now air and food and water didn't matter to him anymore. He thought he could live without them somehow. It was only rage that kept him going.

*Bright Beauty* had been hurt. She would never be the same again.

*Starmaster*'s survivors were going to pay for that. The people who had sent her out against him were going to pay.

Sweating hate, he crossed to the UMCP ship.

Without much trouble, he found an airlock in the intact part of the ship. As soon as he'd entered the lock and closed it behind him, he began to recover. The ship's air pumping into the lock muted the hiss of his tanks. Her survivors might be waiting to ambush him as soon as he came out of the lock—but now at least he was no longer outside, exposed. And inside his rifle would be a devastating weapon.

As the lock cycled open, he ducked to the side, pressed himself against the wall: an instinctive precaution.

His instincts were good. A man stood waiting for him.

At first glance, the man looked all right. His silver hair was rumpled, but that only increased his appearance of eagle authority. Captain's bars marked the shoulders of his tunic. In one fist he held a beam gun.

Angus nearly cried out, "Don't shoot!" even though his suit's transmitter was switched off and his voice would have been inaudible.

"I'm Captain Davies Hyland," the man said. "Angus Thermopyle, you're under arrest." Through the suit's receiver, his confidence sounded insane, detached from reality. "We're going to commandeer your ship."

His eyes hadn't reacted to Angus' movement. He wasn't looking at Angus now. His gun was aimed at the back of the lock.

The parboiled skin around his eyes betrayed what had happened to him.

Flash-blinded in the crash.

In spite of that, he was trying to bluff—

*Commandeer my ship? My SHIP?*

Cackling hideously behind his faceplate, Angus fired. The impact rifle spattered a fine spray of blood thirty meters down the corridor.

Then he hastened to apologize. I'm sorry, Captain Davies Hyland, he said in gleeful courtesy. You can't have my *ship*.

There were a few pieces of the captain's body left on the floor. Angus kicked them out of his way and went looking for the other two survivors. He was starting to feel much better.

The bridge was in this part of *Starmaster*. He went there first—carefully, surveying each corner and passage with his rifle before he risked it, because he had no way to find those two people except by hunting them down. His caution was wasted, however: he didn't see anyone until he reached the bridge. And there the man hunched over the helm console was in no condition to threaten anyone. He was dying where he sat—internal bleeding, Angus guessed. Nothing to worry about.

Angus pushed the man out of his g-seat. New pain made the man cry out; but it also brought his eyes into focus, which was what Angus wanted. Laughing inside his suit, he blasted the man to pulp and splinters, a splash and smear of blood on the floor.

One more to go. Then air filters. Food lockers. A line to the water tanks. And everything else worth taking.

The ship's datacore would have been worth taking, of course. But one look at the bridge computer told him the datacore had already been destructed. Staunch Captain Davies Hyland had probably taken care of that automatically, while his ship was still falling toward the asteroid. So that his precious codes and contacts and orders and even specs wouldn't survive to be used against his masters.

Fuck Captain Davies Hyland, Angus thought. Fuck him everywhere. He's got enough holes in him for that.

Cheered by this observation, Angus pushed a body out of his way and sat down at the scan station. The secondary systems which ran the locks were still operating; that implied parts of the ship still had a bit of juice. This console was one of them. Refocusing short-range scan inward, he used it to locate the last survivor.

There: in a room the scan computer identified as the auxiliary bridge.

That made him snarl under his breath. From the auxiliary bridge, it might still be possible to fire on *Bright Beauty*.

Hurrying now because he knew where his prey was and didn't need caution, he went to finish off the last of *Starmaster*'s crew.

Under the circumstances, his concern for his ship was greater than his desire to inflict pain. He broke into the auxiliary bridge fast with his rifle ready, intending to shoot first and think later.

Morn Hyland stopped him without lifting a finger; without threatening *Bright Beauty;* without so much as reacting to his entrance. Instead, she stared through him with stark, blank horror on her face, as if she could see something so ghastly that it blinded her, making him invisible to her.

In the first few minutes, he didn't even notice his own surprise at finding a woman when he was expecting a man.

Although he knew there was no one else alive on the ship, her fixed stare had the power to turn him around in an effort to see what had appalled her.

Nothing. Of course. She was the only one here. There weren't even any bodies. She'd come through the explosion and the crash without having to watch any of her crewmates die.

Something like a worm of suspicion crawled through Angus Thermopyle's belly. He tightened his grip on his rifle as he confronted her again.

Apparently she still couldn't see him. Her eyes remained nailed to her personal horror, ignoring his movements as if he were too insubstantial to impinge on her vision. She was in shock. If he didn't do anything to help her, she might stay that way for hours. Until something inside her started to heal. Or until she slipped over into madness.

He had no intention whatsoever of helping her.

But then she spoke. In a sore whisper, as if her voice were worn out from screaming, she said, "Let me die."

Inside his suit, Angus had begun to sweat again.

"I don't want help. Let me die. Go away."

He stared at her, studied her. He didn't know it, but his expression resembled hers. Despite its distress, her face had lines that reminded him of Captain Davies Hyland. And the badge on her shipsuit said "Ensign M. Hyland." The captain's daughter? That was quite possible. Ships were often crewed by families. Especially in organizations like the UMCP. Where loyalty was the only thing more important than power and order, muscle and stability, the two essentials of civilization and money. But she looked too young to be a veteran. Her first mission?

"Go away."

What did she see that made her want to die?

Abruptly he keyed his suit's mike. "Why?" Through the speaker, his voice was harsh, like the demanding metal noise of ships in collision. "What did you do to them?"

Without warning, she gripped the sides of her head and began to wail; a thin, weak keening.

"Stop that," he barked. "Tell me what you did to them. If you don't, I'll be glad to beat it out of you."

Her wail cracked, hurt her throat, and scaled higher.

"Shut up!" He brandished his rifle. "They're all dead. Nobody can hear you. I shot your father myself. *Shut up*."

That made her look at him. Some kind of recognition ate into her like acid. For part of a second, she gave him a flare of straight, absolute anguish.

"He survived? He was alive?"

Angus nodded. "Until I blew him apart."

During the space between one heartbeat and the next, she seemed to collapse inward like the core of a fusion reactor, compressing herself for an explosion. Then she flung herself out of her g-seat, clawing at his faceplate.

With her bare hands, she ripped and beat at him, trying to reach him through the suit. Her wail became a screech, as wild as the cry of a mad thing.

At that moment, for no clear or even conscious reason, he took his first step away from himself, his first step along the course which led to his real doom.

He didn't pity her. He didn't pity anybody: any man or woman weak enough to be pitied was weak enough to be taken advantage of. He wasn't ashamed of having killed her father. Captain Davies fornicating Hyland had damaged *Bright Beauty;* he deserved worse than he got. And Angus Thermopyle certainly had no intention of rescuing the captain's daughter. What use could he possibly get out of a madwoman? Never mind the fact that she was UMCP, muscle for all the worlds which had ever despised him, in addition to being a witness to what he had done to that mining camp—a danger to him as long as she lived.

And yet he didn't shoot her.

Maybe he was simply tired of being alone. Maybe on some level he'd begun to notice that behind her fierce distress she was obviously a woman. Maybe his desire to know what had happened to *Starmaster* was stronger than he realized. Or maybe she presented possibilities of revenge which he hadn't yet had a chance to appreciate.

Whatever the reason, when she attacked him he actually dropped his rifle.

For a moment, he grappled with her, fought to pin her arms.

But she was too crazy and frantic for that; so he drew back one heavy fist and clubbed her to the floor.

She whimpered, twisted, tried to squirm away from the pain— and then lay still, breathing in a graceless rasp like the sound of his own respiration inside his suit.

Hitting her—that kind of violence—was so seductive that he wanted to do it again. He wanted to give her ribs a kick and see what would happen. He restrained himself, however. Unexpectedly, he found he had one too many things to worry about. Filters. Supplies. Loot. And her.

And there was always the chance that some other ship was near enough to respond to the distress call he had sent out. *Starmaster* herself may have sent out a distress call. If he were caught here, with a broken UMCP ship to explain, and dead miners not very far away—

Better to forget about her. Forget about looting the ship. Take all the filters and supplies he could get, and leave fast.

Suddenly he was profoundly tired. His suit still had plenty of fresh air; but he'd been hungry and thirsty for several days, and *Starmaster* had nearly killed him. Muttering obscenities at Morn Hyland, hating her because it was all her fault, because she was the only one left of the ship and crew that had made him panic and run as if he were a coward, he slung her over his shoulders and went looking for an EVA locker.

Ominous and slow, like a capped volcano, he suited her, checked her tanks, and carried her against the asteroid's small gravity back to *Bright Beauty*. There he took her into the cubicle of his sickbay. Roughly he strapped her down, so that she couldn't move, and left her, still in her suit because *Bright Beauty*'s air was so foul. Let her come to consciousness alone and not know where she was and be terrified: she deserved it. After pausing to find out what his sniffers and sensors could tell him, he returned to the UMCP ship.

Forcing himself to work long past the point where he wanted to lie down in exhaustion, Angus retrieved his rifle and then set about taking everything that could conceivably be of any value out of *Starmaster*. Enough filters to keep his air clean for years. Food stores of a much higher quality than he would have been willing to pay for. Expensive liquor. Clothes. Spare parts. Medicines. And guns. And tools. Finally he ran a line which allowed him to pump water across to his ship. When he was done, *Bright Beauty* was better supplied than she'd been since the day when he'd first stolen her.

He was wild for rest; but even then he didn't stop. Morn Hyland was awake now. Stripping off his suit, he climbed into his g-seat and turned a receiver to her transmitter so that he could listen to her fear. That kept him going while he lifted off the asteroid and went hunting with glazed eyes and unsteady hands for a place to hide.

He took the first place he found. By then, Morn's voice was stretched and frayed, barely audible; she sounded like she'd lost her mind. He made sure her straps were still secure, shot her full of cat so she wouldn't disturb him. Then he climbed into his bunk and collapsed.

CHAPTER 5

**W**hen he woke up, the air in *Bright Beauty* was so fresh that he could smell himself stink. Too much work. Too much sweat. Too many days in the same shipsuit. Angus Thermopyle wasn't particularly interested in personal cleanliness, but occasionally he felt good enough to take a shower. For some reason, he felt good now. He felt a sense of anticipation.

Munching some of *Starmaster*'s rations, he checked his scan and the computer log to verify that there were no ships anywhere near his hiding place. Then he went to the sickbay to look at Morn Hyland.

She was awake too; the cat had run out of her. When he took off her faceplate, she made a small whimpering noise. "Please." She could hardly force her throat to produce words. "What are you doing? What are you going to do to me?"

He smiled, waved the food bar he was eating, and moved away.

Nearly humming, he stripped, entered the san cubicle, and sprayed himself clean.

Because he was clean—and wearing a fresh shipsuit—when he returned to the sickbay, he was able to tell that Morn herself stank. She'd fouled her suit. Fouled it rather dramatically. Her eyes were raw and dark, full of fear; but he could see in her face that she was still capable of self-disgust.

"You stink," he announced happily.

His tone made her flinch. Apparently the desire to die had been scared out of her.

He looked at her features closely. Just to see what she would do, he ran the tips of his fingers along her cheek. She closed her eyes as if she were fighting a need to vomit.

Grinning, he stepped back. "You hungry?"

She opened her eyes and stared dismay at him.

"Want to get up and move around?"

No answer except dismay.

"Want to get clean?"

That reached her. A tiny hope twisted her mouth, and her eyes filled with tears.

"Good." He folded his arms, rested them on his belly. He was going to enjoy this. "Tell me what you did to them."

She surprised him. Something that looked like anger shone out through her tears; the muscles of her jaw knotted. In a voice so cracked and worn he could hardly hear it, she said, "You bastard. If you're going to kill me, do it. Don't make me lie here like this."

He wanted to hit her. That also would have been enjoyable. But he refrained because he wasn't ready to go that far yet. She was still wearing a suit.

Grinning again, he leaned closer to her and rasped, "You're

right. I'm a bastard. The worst bastard you'll ever meet. And I'm going to let you lie there and *stink* until you tell me what you did to them. You had your guns all lined up. You were going to blast me apart. Then you crashed.

"I want to know why. What did you do?"

The memory hurt her. He was glad to see that. She turned her head as far away as she could inside the EVA suit. Tears dripped past her nose.

Angus sucked his upper lip for a moment, then asked, "What's your name?"

She still didn't speak. Probably trying to be tough. Or maybe she assumed he already knew the answer. After all, he must have seen the badge on her shipsuit.

Roughly he reached one hand to her neck and jerked up her id tag. His computer could have read her entire official file from that tag, but all he wanted was the name.

"Morn Hyland. Captain Davies motherfucking Hyland was your father. That right?"

Now she was crying with her mouth as well as her eyes.

"I shot him. But he was dead anyway." Angus bent over her, whispered in her ear. "His ship crashed. He was going to die no matter what happened. I didn't cause that. I didn't have anything to do with it. It was your doing.

"What did you do to them?"

And she still didn't speak. For the second time, he wanted to hit her. But that could wait. Instead he did something out of character. Without realizing it—entirely without realizing it—he took another small step along the course of his doom. He tried to explain himself.

Almost softly, he said, "You know who I am. What I've got to lose. You know I can't afford to let you loose until I know what

I'm up against. I can't do anything for you until I know what kind of danger you represent."

Almost gently, he returned her tag, then put a hand on her chin and turned her face toward him.

The stark horror was back in her eyes.

Her whisper was faraway and forlorn, lost in darkness. "I initiated self-destruct. From the auxiliary bridge."

His fingers clamped onto her jaw as if he could force her to tell the truth. He thrust his face close to hers. "You did *what*?"

"We were chasing you." Her gaze didn't react to his proximity: the things that appalled her were so bright she couldn't register anything else. "Dodging asteroids. G was awful. I thought we were going to break up. I was at my station. Auxiliary bridge. I thought the straps on my seat were going to tear. Or I was going to rupture.

"Then it stopped.

"I could see you on the screens. But I didn't care. You destroyed that mining camp. I'd already seen you kill all those miners. I didn't care. I should have cared, but I didn't. The whole inside of my head was different.

"I was floating, and everything was clear. Like a vision. It was like the universe spoke to me. I got the message, the truth." Her stare remained fixed; but now she had to fight to keep her sobs down. "The truth.

"I knew exactly what to do. What I had to do. I didn't question it.

"I keyed the self-destruct sequence into the computer. That was supposed to blow up both drives. We would have been turned to powder."

"You aren't an officer," Angus objected. "You're practically a kid. How did you know the self-destruct codes?"

"We all knew the codes. Any one of us could do it. So *Starmaster* wouldn't be captured. That was our first priority. Not be captured. Under any circumstances. If forbidden space got us—a ship like that— We can all be trusted. We're all reliable. Most of us are family. They wouldn't let anybody who wasn't reliable on a ship like that.

"But fa—Captain Hyland caught what I was doing. He tried to abort. Only the thrusters exploded. I could hear him yelling at me over the intercom—yelling at me because I was his daughter and I was destroying his ship, I was destroying him. His sister and brothers. My cousins. Destroying them.

"And then it wasn't clear anymore. There wasn't any vision. We weren't in any danger. It was all a lie. I killed my whole family for no reason."

Fighting to contain her grief, she did her desperate best to shout, *"Get me out of this suit!"*

He ignored the demand. "Stop whining. Let me think." Suddenly he was sure of his suspicions. He'd taken a maniac aboard *Bright Beauty,* a human time bomb. And yet it didn't make sense.

"How many times have you crossed the gap?"

"Twice," she answered, cowed not by his irritation but by her own despair.

"Twice," he echoed viciously. "Of course. Cops like you have to be deep-space certified. So they test you in the Academy. To weed out the crazies who get gap-sickness. And then you had to reach Com-Mine Station. You've only crossed the gap twice because this is your first deep-space assignment. It doesn't make *sense.*"

But while he was still speaking, he guessed the truth. Gap-sickness came in every conceivable shape and disguise. He had heard of people who crossed the gap once—or even several times—and then lived perfectly normal lives until the right stimuli came along, until the right combination of circumstances occurred to trigger their personal vulnerability, their peculiar flaw.

Combat? G-stress?

"How many times"—he took hold of her face again, forced her gaze toward him—"have you been under heavy g since the first time you crossed the gap?"

She gaped at him, anguish changing into comprehension in her eyes.

"*Answer* me. You did all kinds of g work in the Academy. They trained you for everything they could think of. Did you do that before or after your first gap crossing? When was the last time you were under heavy g?"

"Before," she husked weakly. Her voice seemed to stick in her teeth. "The gap comes last. Only if you want to crew in deep space. Earth can't afford to risk people who want to work in-system. Can't risk wasting all that training and expense for people who aren't going to be in any danger."

She must have understood what he was getting at, because she concluded with thin, cracked lucidity, "Chasing you was the first time I've been under heavy g since before my first crossing."

"Great. Wonderful." Angus tried a few obscenities, but they seemed inadequate. "Bitch. I never should have rescued you. I must have been out of my mind. It's not bad enough you're a fucking cop. And a witness. It's not bad enough you're going to turn me in the first chance you get. On top of that, you're going to go crazy and try to kill me as soon as we hit heavy g." He gouged his fingers into the sides of her face, then released her. "I should have left you to die."

Again she surprised him. Her gaze steadied, and her voice gave an improbable suggestion of strength, of sarcasm. "It's not too late. You can still kill me. No one will ever know."

A smile stretched his features, making him look more than ever like a malign frog. He wasn't accustomed to the way he felt: happy; eager. She might turn out to be exactly what he needed.

"If I did that," he replied, "I wouldn't have a crew."

"*Crew?*" The idea seemed to focus her stubbornness. "I'm not going to crew for you. I'm not—"

Yet in spite of what she felt, her voice trailed away. He wasn't paying any attention to her refusal.

Deliberately, obviously, so that she could watch everything, he instructed the sickbay computer to prepare an anesthetic and pump it into her. While the needle probed her veins, he savored her dismay.

As she lost consciousness, she breathed in appeal, "Get me out of this—"

"Oh, I will," he promised. "I will."

If he'd been that kind of man, he would have chuckled.

Thanks to the advances of medical technology, even *Bright Beauty*'s tiny sickbay was well-enough-equipped to administer a zone implant.

He had to unstrap her in order to get her head and shoulders out of the suit. That was the hard part, hampered as he was by her dead weight and the confines of the cubicle. The rest was simple. All he had to do was tell the sickbay computer what he wanted and then get out of the way. Cybernetic systems took care of the rest.

Long ago, he'd disconnected the sickbay computer from his ship's datacore. Law-abiding ships had that right, to protect the privacy of their passengers and crew: as long as the sickbay computer didn't feed directly to the datacore, no permanent record was kept of who needed treatment and why; so private citizens didn't need to worry that their medical records would be used against them. After all, crucial information—such as the presence of gap-sickness—was recorded on id tags. And any captain could add data to anyone's id file as necessary. However, Angus' intentions had nothing to do with abiding by the law. He simply wanted to neutralize his sickbay computer as a source of evidence against him.

In fact, he'd carried his precautions to the extent of programming the computer with an automatic erase, so that it immediately "forgot" every treatment it dispensed, every procedure it performed. According to his official sickbay log, he was the only person who had ever been aboard *Bright Beauty*—and he had never used his sickbay.

Confident of his own security, he left the cybernetic systems alone while they worked on Morn Hyland, preparing her for his use.

Instead of watching what was done to her, he lifted *Bright Beauty* gently out of hiding and went in search of a better covert, a place where he could feel safe for the time it would take to train his crew. Before long he found the kind of asteroid he liked: played-out and deserted, riddled with abandoned tunnels and workings which would attract nobody. Deep in one of the old mine shafts, out of reach of any ordinary scan, he parked his ship. Just in case he lost control of what he was doing, he shut down her drive and locked everything in the command module with priority codes. Then he went to check on his patient.

The sickbay computer was done with her: in fact, it had already washed the anesthetic out of her body, and she was starting to wake up. He just had time to pick up the implant control and make sure it was functioning properly before she began to stir, moving her arms groggily and blinking her eyes.

"You stink," he said before she was altogether able to understand him. "Go get clean."

With an effort, she got her eyes into focus. At the same time, she seemed to realize that her limbs were free—that he had undone the straps. She frowned at him, struggling to think. Reflexively, she pulled her legs up, stretched her arms.

"What're you doing?" Her voice sounded rusty, as if she hadn't used it for a long time. "Why did you put me to sleep?"

Watching her closely, he rasped, "I said, you stink. Go get clean."

"Yes, sir." She was fresh from the Academy: assent to authority still came naturally. Her gaze blurred, and her nose wrinkled as she smelled the mess she had made in the suit. Carefully she swung her legs over the edge of the surgery berth, eased herself into a sitting position. Just for a second, he thought she was actually going to thank him for the opportunity to use the sanitary cubicle.

But movement helped clear her head. Her frown sharpened. Gripping the edge of the berth to steady herself, she looked at him again. "Why am I free? Why did you put me to sleep?"

He bared his teeth. "I told you. You're my crew now. You're mine. You've been *impressed.*" He relished the word. "When I tell you to do something, I expect it done."

He could see suspicion mounting to panic in her face. "You bastard," she breathed for the second time. "I'm not your crew. I'm UMCP. I'm going to leave you rotting in lockup if it's the last thing I do. *What have you done to me?*"

Angus didn't answer directly: he was having too much fun. Instead, he showed her the control in his hand.

The shock when she recognized the small box was everything he could have wanted. It was like her horror of the way she had murdered her family, like that in helplessness and extremity; and yet profoundly different in other, crucial respects. Terror and loathing burned across her face. Her hands sprang to her mouth; she made an attempt to cry out.

Then she hurled herself at him.

Unhindered by the asteroid's negligible gravity, she came at him like a crazy. In her frenzy, she was so wild that she looked rabid—frantic enough to tear him apart.

But he had good reflexes. They'd often saved his life. And as a matter of instinct he was already braced against the bulkhead, ready. He shoved himself to the side, moving almost as fast as she did.

At the same time, he pushed one of the main function buttons on the zone-implant control.

That one was for emergencies: it was intended to save the people around her from her fits of gap-sickness after everything else failed. When he pushed it, she went instantly catatonic.

Limp as an empty shipsuit, she collided with the bulkhead and flopped backward. The asteroid's small tug pulled her down slowly, so that she fell like a grotesque feather against the edge of the surgery berth and settled toward the floor.

"You *stink!*" Angus raged at her, squeezing the control triumphantly. "Go get clean. When I tell you to do something, *I expect it done.*"

She could hear him: he knew she could hear him. Her eyes retained the color of consciousness. That was the blessing—or the curse—of the zone implant's cataleptic function. It didn't affect her mind: it only short-circuited the connection between what her mind wanted and what her body did. She could hear him; yet she lay on the floor in a heap of flaccid limbs. If he'd taken a welding torch to her belly, she wouldn't have reacted in any way.

Her state wasn't particularly rewarding for him, however. After a moment, he keyed off the control. At once, a spasm ran through all her muscles, making her twitch like an epileptic.

Helpless to do anything else, she burst into a fury of tears.

Once again, she seemed to find a chink in his character, a small way in which he was unlike himself. He let her cry for a little while, gave her a chance to understand his power over her. Then, almost without gloating, he said, "You had enough? Go get clean. Down there." He pointed along the passage toward the san and the head.

She flinched as if he'd tried to put a hand on her. Hugging herself against the bulkhead, she looked up at him. So thinly that he could hardly hear her, she asked, "What do you want from me? You'll get the death penalty for this. You might be able to get off with life imprisonment for what you did to those miners. You might be able to convince a court you had some kind of reason—or you were just crazy. But you can't get away with this. Nobody ever gets away with 'unauthorized use of a zone implant.' Why are you doing it?"

Without warning, he felt vulnerable to her—violent and angry. But he still didn't hit her. Because of the chink she'd found in him, his answer was simple. "I need a crew. How else can I get a gap-sick cop to crew for me?"

Eventually she nodded, as if what he said made sense.

With misery in her eyes, struggling visibly against her fear, she got to her feet and did what he told her. She went past him down the corridor.

For no reason he could explain—no reason he knew—he handed her a clean shipsuit before she entered the san.

By the time she emerged, however, the inexplicable inconsistency of his own behavior had made him savage. He was a coward; and when he did things he didn't understand, things that weren't what he'd intended, things that weren't what he wanted, he scared himself. When he was scared, he took action.

He was being weak. He should have forced her to live in that fouled suit in order to humiliate her properly, teach her what his power meant. What was he doing? Was he feeling sorry for her? The idea made him want to break her arms. He would see her dead— he would *crush* her—before he would allow her to do anything that might make him weak.

And yet he contained himself until she came out of the san of her own volition. Fuming, fretting, swelling into a fury, he still waited, storing up violence, until she opened the door herself and came out to face him.

Then he lost his self-possession.

He was already on the edge of his restraint: the sight of her pushed him past his limits. She was clean—and being clean brought back her fundamental beauty. She was probably the most beautiful woman he'd ever seen this close. And she showed a kind of courage simply by leaving the san; she had the capacity to face her fate. Her eyes shone with a heart-wrenching combination of fright and de-fiance, with a dread of what he could do to her mixed with a refusal to be cowed. And he could do anything he wanted. She was his: he had the control to her zone implant clenched in his sweating fingers.

For that reason, he pushed the button which took away her ability to move. Then he put down the control and beat her bloody with his bare fists, marring her beauty so that it wouldn't terrify him anymore.

CHAPTER

**S**everal hours passed before he came to the realization that he'd hurt himself as well as her.

With the zone-implant control, of course, he could have over-ridden the damage to some extent. As soon as she regained any measure of consciousness, he could have forced her into motion, made her serve him in any number of ways. Certainly he could have muffled the sensations of damage for her. But she would still have been useless as crew: he had left her in no condition to learn the things he needed to teach her about *Bright Beauty*. He would have to give her time to recover before he could get any real use out of her.

In other words, he'd increased the amount of time he would have to spend in hiding. He'd delayed the moment when he would be able—if not safe—to travel with Morn's help instead of hindrance. And no matter how well hidden he was, the fact remained that a stationary target was easier to find and hit than a moving one.

He'd increased the risk to himself for the satisfaction of beating her.

And he'd hurt himself in another, subtler way as well. She was *his*. Wasn't she? Like his ship, she was in his command. With the zone implant, he could make her do anything he wanted; perhaps by taking control of her body and directing it as he wished; perhaps by exerting neural pressure—pain and pleasure strong enough to coerce her. He could make her (now that she was unconscious and out of sight, his imagination began to tease him) do *that*. He could do *that* to her. So why was he afraid of her looks? Beauty only made it better—only increased her humiliation, demonstrated his power more completely. Anything that marred her took something away from him.

He was so surprised—in a sense, so shaken—by this perception that he went to her without thinking, carried her back into the sickbay, and instructed the computer to treat her injuries.

Another step.

Soon his surprise became a visceral trembling, an ague in the core of his distended gut. New ideas were working on him. He wasn't thinking about revenge now—about having a UMC cop as his crew, about making her suffer for what *Starmaster* had done to *Bright Beauty*. Now his thoughts were more visceral. He'd never had much to do with women. In the course of his piracies, he'd captured or kidnapped a few, used them hard, then gotten rid of them. But none of them had had Morn Hyland's capacity to make him shiver, make him do things he didn't expect. None of them had been so entirely in his possession—or so desirable.

She was still unconscious, perhaps because of his beating, perhaps because of the drugs the sickbay computer gave her. She had no idea what was happening as he undid her shipsuit and peeled it off her limbs.

He couldn't stop trembling. After all, it was a good thing that he'd hit her. The darkness and swelling of her bruises made her bearable: if she'd remained perfect, he would have had no choice but to kill her. So he paid no attention to the firm lift of her breasts or the velvet curve of her hips. He concentrated exclusively on the livid hurt of her bruises as he climbed on top of her.

His orgasm was so intense that he thought for a moment he'd broken something.

Before he rolled off her, he had the satisfaction of seeing her eyes flutter open, seeing her begin to realize what he'd done. He filled her with revulsion, even though there was nothing she could do about it. That was good.

Nevertheless he continued trembling.

He could no longer tell whether he was excited or afraid.

"Does that make you feel like a man?" She sounded bitter and miserable—and faraway, as though the aftereffects of his blows muffled her distress. "Do you have to destroy me to feel good yourself? Are you that sick?"

"Shut up," he replied amiably. "You'll get used to it. You'll have to." He was grinning; but he still had to brace his hands on his hips to conceal the way they shook.

As if she hadn't heard him—as if she were still on the same subject—she muttered, "It's because of men like you I became a cop."

It occurred to him that what he was doing to her might make her come apart. Maybe she had already begun. At the idea, he bared his teeth.

"Is that so?" he drawled. "I thought it was because you like guns. Muscle. They make *you* feel like a man."

Maybe she was still stupefied by blows and rape and medication: maybe she didn't hear him. Or maybe she really was trying to threaten him. "Forbidden space is bad enough. We don't need any worse threats than that. But men like you are worse. You betray your own kind. You prey on human beings—on human survival—and get rich." She didn't look at him. Perhaps if she had looked at him she would have lost the courage for what she was saying. "I'll do anything I can to stop you," she recited like an article of faith. "No price is too high for stopping a man like you."

Angus had to respond. Involuntarily he remembered the insane bravado with which blind Captain Davies Hyland had tried to out-face him. He couldn't let the captain's daughter think he cared about her threats.

"Me?" he retorted, gathering anger or pleasure as he spoke. "I'm a danger to human space? What about you? I wasn't the one who blew up your ship. I didn't make you gap-sick. I didn't hunt you down. I didn't even fire on you. You killed all those cops yourself, *you*." This was fun. He was going to teach her what her threats were good for. "I'm just a freighter captain. You're a traitor."

He could see his words hit her: she winced and turned her head away. As if he'd switched her off—or as if she were trying to find some hidden place where she could still believe in herself—she seemed to sink out of awareness.

Where she went, he couldn't follow. For him, fear was a source of inspiration: it enabled him to make the sort of intuitive leap which had brought him to an understanding of her gap-sickness. But the same inspiration or intuition also blinded him to perceptions which involved emotions other than fear.

The place where Morn went would have made no sense to him. He would have assumed it was a cynical lie—the kind of falsehood which conceals itself in order to sting more effectively.

She was sinking down to her basic memories, to the place where she had become who she was; to her home and parents.

Like a little girl, unselfconsciously, she appealed to her mother and father for help.

In a sense, their power to help or hinder her, like their power to shape her life, came from the fact that they'd been so much absent. They were both cops; and the UMCP policy of crewing ships with families stopped short of children. In consequence, Morn was left with her grandparents (themselves retired veterans of Space Mines Inc. Security) while Davies and Bryony Hyland served missions in the deep void, risking their lives to protect humankind from violence and forbidden space.

Morn kept the weight of this abandonment to herself. Of course, she grieved when they went away; she thrilled with joy when they returned. But the deeper impact she concealed. Perhaps she herself didn't know there was any deeper impact. After all, her parents left her in a home where she was loved and attended to; a home where a strict affirmation of law and citizenship was complemented by warmth and affection. For her grandparents, as for her parents, children were the future which the UMCP labored and bled to secure.

Virtually everyone Morn knew as a child either was or had been a cop. And they were *believers:* they esteemed their own work in the same way that they esteemed her, and for the same reason. They spoke of her parents with a fundamental respect, an unquestioning validation, which taught her that what her mother and father did was the most necessary and valuable job imaginable. Life beyond the hegemony of the UMCP thronged with profound perils, threats to the human species itself, which Davies and Bryony Hyland had the courage and the conviction to oppose. Vast space was deadly: it called for valor, determination, and idealism.

How could a child question all this? Whom could she tell that she felt abandoned—or punished? By the time she was old enough to know the right words, they were no longer credible. Abandonment? Punishment? No. She'd been taught to see her father as an eagle, scouring the skies for predators. And her mother was a panther, sleek and soft for her kittens, but ready with fangs and claws to fight her kittens' enemies.

In addition, her grandparents, aunts, uncles—and her parents when they were on leave—conveyed the perfect assumption that Morn herself would eventually become a cop. Precisely because she was bright, capable, and loved, she would naturally choose to follow in her parents' footsteps.

Morn nodded solemnly, as if she were accepting her mission. Nevertheless she knew it was false. She would never be a cop. When the pain of her abandonment or punishment lost credibility, she learned resentment. But there was no place for that in her life, so it remained hidden. Instead of aspiring to be like her parents, she learned to hold a grudge.

Even at that age, she was able to hold a grudge steadily—and give no sign of it.

However, her resentment turned to shame—her whole emotional makeup changed—when she heard of her mother's death.

Of course her grandparents were the first to tell her that Bryony had been killed. But in her core, where her image of her mother's invincibility resided, she didn't believe the news until she heard it from her father. He came home on leave after the ship which he had served as first officer, the UMCP cruiser *Intransigent,* limped to the haven of Orion's Reach. As soon as his debriefing at UMCPHQ permitted, he sat down with Morn and told her the story.

She saved us all, he said. She'll be given the Medal of Valor for it. He must have assumed that Morn would want to know this. If she hadn't sacrificed herself, we would all have been lost.

He held his daughter on his lap with his arms around her as he talked. Under the circumstances, she wasn't too old for this. His voice was steady and clear—the voice of a man who valued what his wife had done too much to protest against it. Yet tears ran from his eyes, collected along the certainty of his jaw, and dropped like stains onto Morn's small breast.

We picked up a distress call from the ore transfer dump off Orion's Reach. The dump was raided. An illegal came in on them hard, blasted most of the habitation and control centers, then took all the ore that was ready for shipping and headed away. They would probably have been safe if the illegal had known we were in the vicinity. But no one knew. We were hunting. We didn't advertise our movements.

We left medical supplies and personnel at the dump and took off after the illegal.

She called herself *Gutbuster*. She wasn't fast, and she didn't show gap capability. But she was heavily armed—as heavily armed as a battlewagon. We'd never heard of her before. We didn't know there were any illegal ships that powerful. We were only a day of hard g away from Orion's Reach when we engaged her. But by the time we drove her off, we were so badly damaged that we couldn't get back for a week.

Of course, we ordered her to come about. We told her she was under arrest. And we didn't charge in recklessly. We could tell by her particle trace that she was something we hadn't seen before, so we were cautious. But she kept on running, ignoring us. Finally we had to attack.

We were careful—but we should have been more careful. We were too sure of ourselves. And too angry at what *Gutbuster* did to the dump. And we're cops, Morn. We're the police. We can't simply destroy illegals without giving them every conceivable chance to surrender. If we did that, we wouldn't be any better than the people we're fighting.

Because we weren't careful enough, and because we gave her too much chance to surrender, her first blast ripped one whole side of *Intransigent* open as if we had no shielding, and had never heard of evasive maneuvers.

A pure super-light proton beam. It was no wonder she was slow. Every bit of energy she could produce must have been necessary to power that cannon. Captain Davies Hyland couldn't resist lecturing for a moment. That's why UMCP cruisers don't use them. We need mobility and speed. We can't afford the kind of energy-utilization priorities those cannon require.

I was on the bridge. The bridge wasn't hit. But that blast did us so much damage that we immediately lost targ. The cables were cut. We still had power, but we couldn't aim our guns. Another beam like that would have finished us. As it was, the only reason we survived was that *Gutbuster* needed time to recharge her cannon.

Your mother was on station in targeting control. And targeting control was in the part of *Intransigent* that *Gutbuster* hit. All the control spaces were close to the core, of course. But that whole side of *Intransigent* had been ripped open to vacuum. Even your mother's station lost structural integrity. A bulkhead cracked, welds parted. Targeting control began to lose atmosphere.

She could have saved herself—for a minute or two, anyway. The leak was slow enough. She could have left her station, sealed it behind her. The automatic systems that locked the doors had enough override tolerance for that. But she didn't. Instead, she stayed at her board. While her station depressurized and her air ran out, she worked to reroute targ function so that we could use our guns.

She succeeded, Morn. That's why *Intransigent* survived, why I'm here talking to you. She restored targ in time. We hit *Gutbuster* with everything we had. And because *Gutbuster* needed power to maneuver, she couldn't use her proton beam again. We fought until she couldn't stand any more damage. Then she pulled away.

But your mother was lost. By the time she finished saving us, the automatic locks wouldn't let her out of targeting control. Depressurization exceeded their tolerances.

You know how people die in vacuum, Morn. It isn't pretty. But it's beautiful to me, as beautiful as your mother herself. She gave her life for her shipmates. If I die that way myself someday, I'll die proud.

And I promise you this. Now the look of an eagle shone through Davies Hyland's tears, as familiar as his certainty and his strong arms. No one in the UMCP will ever rest until your mother has been avenged. We will stop *Gutbuster* and every ship like her. We will stop every illegal who sells out humanity.

By the time his story ended, Morn had decided that she, too, would be a cop. She was too ashamed of herself to make any other choice. She already felt—an emotion which lost credibility as soon as it was put into words—that she'd killed her mother with her secret grudge. So she told herself that she owed it to human space, to her father, to the image of her mother, and to herself to join those who opposed the betrayal of humankind. But those were only words. The truth was that she was trying to recant.

However, it was a matter of historical record that *Gutbuster* was never stopped. Morn learned this during her years in the UMCP Academy. Indeed, that ship was never encountered again. She died of her wounds in the void; or found the problematic safety of forbidden space and never returned; or transformed herself in some way (perhaps by replacing her datacore), changed her registration and codes so that she couldn't be recognized. The promise Morn received from her father was never kept.

At the time, in the Academy, she took that failure as a reason to rededicate herself to her calling. If *Gutbuster* and similar ships still existed, perhaps flourished, then people like Morn were needed more than ever; people who had both reason for passion and experience to give their passion focus. She made herself one of the best cadets in her class—an honor to her father, and to her mother's memory. If she had any questions about what she was doing—if she felt any uncertainty about her father, or the UMCP, or about her own courage—she kept that hidden, even from herself.

By the time she joined *Starmaster* and Captain Davies Hyland in their quest to preserve the integrity of human space, any doubts she might have retained were hidden so deep that only a man like Angus Thermopyle could have dredged them up.

But she'd killed her father. She'd brought what was left of her family to ruin.

That struck her in the deepest part of her shame—in the part which believed she'd deserved to be abandoned; the part which believed her resentment had killed her mother.

When she needed them most—helpless in *Bright Beauty*'s sickbay, with a zone implant in her head and Angus leering over her—her parents didn't answer her appeal.

How could they? Nothing they'd ever given her or done for her had prepared her for the crisis of gap-sickness; for the knowledge that the destructive flaw which endangered those she loved existed, not in illegals and forbidden space, but in herself.

The look in her eyes as she came back from her search for courage was one of unmitigated and irremediable anguish.

"Even if I can't do it," she said as if her heart were hollow, "somebody else will. It doesn't matter what you think of me. Maybe you're right. Maybe I'm as bad as a traitor. But there are better cops than me—stronger— They'll stop you. They'll make you pay for this."

Her throat closed. The glaze across her eyes was fading. She began to look sharper, more dangerous; her nipples were poised on her breasts as if they could do damage.

Instinctively, Angus put his hand in his pocket, closed his fingers around the control. His grip was damp with sweat.

But she was wrong. He had no doubt that she was wrong. Oh, the fucking cops would stop him if they could. They would gut his ship and kill him gladly. But not because of what he did to her—or to those miners. Reasons like that were only excuses, as empty as her tone. The UMCP didn't protect people. Why should it? It protected money. It protected itself. It protected the power to despise people like Angus himself.

The cops would try to stop and kill him, not because he shed blood, but because he cut into UMC profits.

Under the circumstances, he had no idea why he'd left her alone so long; why he'd given her time to go looking for courage. He didn't have any reason for it. Nevertheless he was either excited or angry; and that confusion held him. And he had the control to her zone implant in his pocket: he was secure. Let her find courage, if she could. The braver she was, the more pleasure he would get out of breaking her.

When he thought about breaking her, he grew erect again.

Instead of arguing with her, he removed his hand from his

pocket. A twitch of his fists parted the seals on his shipsuit, allowing him to jut out.

"They'll never get the chance," he rasped, showing his yellow teeth. "I told you. I'm a bastard. The worst bastard you'll ever meet. And I'm good at what I do. I've been dancing circles around the fucking cops all my life. If they ever catch me, it'll be long after you're dead.

"In the meantime, I'm going to have some fun with you. You're my crew now. You're going to learn to take orders. And I've got old scores to settle. A lot of them. I'm going to settle them on you. By the time I'm done, you're going to want to run away so bad it'll damn near kill you, but I won't even let you scream."

She glanced down at his crotch. Her mouth betrayed an unmistakable desire to wail. And yet she fought not to let him appall her. Her withdrawal may not have brought her courage; nevertheless she possessed a strength of her own which had never been tested before. Her voice shook as she said, "If nobody else stops you, I'll have to do it. I'll get the chance somehow. I can't fight a zone implant. You've got that on your side. But I can't crew for you while you're keeping me passive. You'll have to let me move on my own—think on my own. I'll get the chance."

Her defiance was secretly disturbing—and secretly stimulating. He wanted to hit her again; but he knew that would be an inferior pleasure. To crush her spirit would give him a positive joy. Furthermore, it was necessary. She was right: she wouldn't be able to crew for him under the control of the zone implant. The requirements of the job were too complex—and the functions of her implant were too crude. If he had to tell her what to do all the time, she would be useless. If he needed her help with *Bright Beauty*, he would be vulnerable. He wouldn't be able to leave his hiding place until he was sure she was broken.

And yet her spirit was part of what made her so desirable.

He didn't hesitate, however. He'd already taken too many steps in a direction he didn't understand. Still jutting from the seam of his shipsuit, he took out the implant control and snapped it on.

Helpless to resist, she lapsed into a pliant state similar to hypnosis; a state in which she could no longer choose her own movements.

He had to swallow several times to moisten his throat. As he tapped buttons on the control, he rasped, "Sit up."

Eyes disfocused, features slack, she sat up on the edge of the berth.

He reached into one of the compartments along the bulkhead, selected a scalpel, and handed it toward her. "Take it."

Her fingers closed involuntarily. Only the darkness in her gaze hinted that she knew what she was doing.

He had to clench his fists to keep himself still. He was approaching orgasm again. "Put the edge on your tit."

The control compelled her. She didn't need to watch what she was doing. Blindly she moved the scalpel until the blade rested against her nipple, intense silver against brown. The nipple was erect and hard, as if it were ready to be cut.

"You can understand me," he said thickly. "I know you can, so pay attention. I can make you cut yourself. If I want to, I can make you cut off your whole tit." He was tempted to have her draw blood, just to demonstrate his power; but he was afraid if he did so he would come right away. "Remember that when you think about breaking my neck.

"I'm going to break *you*. I'm going to break you so hard you'll start to love it, need it. Then I'm going to break you some more. I'm going to break you until you don't have anything but me to live for."

Her eyes were still out of focus; but he could see anguish in their depths, a wail she was unable to utter.

She looked so lost that he almost turned off the zone implant. It would be an exquisite display of possession to make her do what he wanted by plain fear rather than with the implant—to make her return the scalpel to its compartment, then come to him, kneel in front of him, and open her mouth so that he could thrust himself down her throat. His thumb was on the switch to release her.

But at the last moment, instinct prevailed. He couldn't take the risk of ignoring her threats. She might be stronger than he could predict. If she was— The idea took some of the stiffness out of him.

Angrily, he kept her under control.

Moving like a robot—responsive to nothing but the implant's functions—she replaced the scalpel in its compartment. When he instructed her to smile, she obeyed; but the lift of her lips remained as expressionless as the rest of her face. Obediently she knelt in front of him.

His organ was no longer as intensely eager as it had been a few moments ago. Down in the black bottom of his heart, he was disappointed. His cowardice had cost him something he wanted. But disappointment made him angry—and anger had its uses. Suddenly furious, he forced open her mouth and drove himself into her, gagging her fiercely until he came.

Then a sense of depletion as sudden as his rage took everything else away. Without a glance at her, he pushed the buttons which put her to sleep; he left her naked on the floor of the sickbay. Thinking he was tired, he lumbered away toward his berth to get some rest.

But he wasn't tired. What he felt wasn't fatigue: it was loss. After several restless minutes, he left his berth and went, fuming bitterly, to *Bright Beauty*'s bridge and the command console. There he keyed on the cameras and screens so that he could look at the damage *Starmaster* had done to his ship.

She had a cabin-size dent in her side. Her steel skeleton was no longer true. One part of her nose looked like it'd been hit by an impact-ram.

She could be repaired. He knew where to go to get her patched and welded and sealed: fixed. But she would never be the same again.

As he studied her wounds, Angus Thermopyle's eyes began to spill tears.

CHAPTER 7

$\mathbf{F}$rom that point on, he no longer hit Morn Hyland. She was his, and he was ready, eager, to use her hard; but he didn't want her damaged.

Driven by anger and grief, and by a vague, inexplicable sense that he was no longer in control of his life, he used her so hard that several days passed before he could begin teaching her how to help him with *Bright Beauty*. He'd never had much to do with women. In fact, he'd never doubted that he could live perfectly well without them altogether. But now his brain teemed with lust. Perversions which had never occurred to him before now seemed exciting, even compulsory. The more he saw of her helpless beauty, and the more he exercised himself on her flesh, the greater her hold on his imagination became—the more power she seemed to have over him.

It was madness to stay where he was: stationary, hidden, defenseless. He should have been on his way to the nearest bootleg shipyard days ago. It was weeks away under hard boost, inside the borders of forbidden space, where cops never went; he should have gotten started immediately. But he kept thinking of things he could do to Morn—of ways to enjoy her imposed compliance—of outlets for his most intimate and personal rage. The firm line of her thighs and the soft pillow of her belly haunted his dreams: he was kept awake by the way her breasts lifted to him despite the intensity of her loathing. For several days, he was simply unable to think about anything else.

Finally, during one of the periods when he released her from the zone implant's control so that he could take a look at her despair, abhorrence, nausea—look at them and savor them—she asked, "Why are you doing this? Why do you hate me so much?"

They were in the sickbay because its berth was easier to use than any of the others. She sat on the floor, against the bulkhead, with her legs hugged to her chest in misery and her face hidden between her knees. He'd seen sewer rats on Com-Mine Station and elsewhere, derelicts, nerve-juice addicts, even null-wave transmitters, with more energy and hope than she showed. She was breaking, as he'd promised she would. Already it seemed impossible that she would ever have the courage to threaten him again.

And yet she was still groping—still reaching for something—

"Why are you doing this? Why do you hate me so much?"

She was like *Bright Beauty:* she had surprises in her.

"What difference does it make?" he growled, just for something to say. "How come you're the one with gap-sickness, instead of me? Who knows? Who cares? I've *got* you. That's all there is."

She lifted her head a little: her eyes showed, black as rot and ruin, past her kneecaps. Her voice twitched as if she were afraid or crazy. "You can do better than that."

He sucked his upper lip, thinking casually. For some reason, he felt expansive, almost magnanimous. It was possible that she was crazy. Possessiveness warmed him as if it were a species of affection.

Abruptly he said, "All right. I'll tell you something about me. A little story to help you understand." He was sneering. "I had a roommate once."

Morn Hyland stared at him without any reaction at all.

"Back on Earth," he explained. "In reform school. I was a snot-nose kid—didn't know enough to keep them from catching me. Fuckers. Caught me helping myself in a foodvend. But of course they didn't care I was doing it because I was *hungry*. All they cared about was reforming me. Make me 'a productive member of society.' Break me. So they locked me up in school.

"I hated it. One thing I promised. Nobody is ever going to lock me up again—"

That was a digression, however: Angus had no wish to think about being locked up. If he did, he would lose his present sense of indulgence and fall into a fury. Over the years, he'd done some desperate things—reckless things, things that probably made him look brave. But courage had nothing to do with them. He'd done them to escape the danger of being locked up.

"I had a roommate," he resumed. "They told me I was lucky I only had one. Crowded three or four into a room was more like it. But it wasn't luck. They put me alone with that shithead because they thought he'd be good for me.

"They were all *cops*." The taste of their power over him made him want to spit. "Like you. They talked about protecting and reforming, but what they really liked was muscle. Just like you. Muscle to kill me. Or break me—it's the same thing. I was just a street rat who got caught raiding a foodvend. I couldn't defend myself. They thought they could beat me.

"My roommate was supposed to be a good example. One of their big successes. They got him for lifting paper from his step-father's wallet, and after only five years in reform school he was on the path of virtue. They wanted him to help reform me.

"His name was Scarl. He was a big fucker—the kind of illegal who eats shit and smiles. Lots of teeth. He wanted to *reform* me, for sure. Anything to make himself look good. He already figured out the way to beat them was be their little darling, make them think he was sugar—make them take care of him. I was his big chance to show off.

"It was pathetic. He sure did want me to believe he was my friend. So he made a big deal out of taking care of me. Taught me how the school worked. Didn't let the big shits pound me. Showed me how to get perks—how to lift treats—how to be on the nice-kid list. After a whole day of him every day, I wanted to puke.

"But I got him." Angus had arrived at the part of the memory he liked. "I got him. Good old Scarl never knew what hit him.

"We had lockers. It was supposed to be good for kids to have something private. Everybody hid the keys, like what was in the lockers was precious. But he wasn't good at hiding things. I took his.

"Then I raided some of their rooms, the cops'. Lifted a bunch of small stuff—vials of nerve-juice, fancy pens, whatever I found. And one of them had a really great collection of dirty pictures." He bared his teeth at Morn. "That's where I still get most of my ideas."

She didn't react, however.

"I put it all in Scarl's locker, locked it up. Then I put his key back. He never missed it.

"Next morning they went crazy. They stormed into all our rooms. Made us give up our keys and stand there naked until they got around to searching our lockers.

"When he saw all that stuff in his locker, good old Scarl fainted."

Angus forced a guffaw, but it wasn't particularly successful. For some reason, the pleasure of what he'd done to Scarl had lost its flavor. There was a bitter taste in his mouth, as if someone had cheated him.

Trying to muster relish for his story, he concluded, "Those dirty pictures finished him. They were too embarrassing for the school. He got shipped out. Maybe they sent him to the big boys' lockup." Unfortunately, he felt no relish. "I got put in a room with a bunch of motherfuckers who liked to cornhole me when they didn't have anything better to do.

"It was like that until I finally got a chance to break out and get away."

Her stare hadn't shifted. She was still peering at him darkly over her kneecaps, still waiting. When he stopped, she watched him scowl for a while. Then she asked, "What does that have to do with me?"

"Huh?" He'd forgotten her question.

"You betrayed your roommate." Her voice was husky with the stress of all the things he'd done to her. "But he was the one who protected you. Betraying him probably hurt you worse than it did him. What does it have to do with me?"

Cursing the loss of his expansive mood, Angus sealed his shipsuit. "It felt good. That's what it has to do with you. It felt good."

He started to leave in disgust; his back was turned when she said softly, thinly, "Stop this."

He paused.

"So far you've got 'authorized use.' For this zone implant. I'll testify to that. I'll say you had to do it. To save both of us. Just stop this. Just stop."

Angus turned to look at her, but now she was not looking at him.

"What happened to being a cop? What happened to all those threats? I thought you were going to find some way to do me in."

"I'm afraid," she murmured as if she were pleading. "I want to live."

The way she clutched her knees and hid her features suddenly gave him the impression she'd come face-to-face with an essential cowardice.

"I'll crew for you back to Com-Mine Station. I'll testify—I'll say you did the right thing. They'll believe me. I'm UMCP. I won't say anything about those miners. I'll"—her voice caught, but she forced herself to go on—"I'll do whatever you want. I'll be your lover. Just so you stop. Stop hurting me."

For one strange moment, Angus found himself listening to her as if he could be persuaded—as if she had the power to make him pity her. Had he broken her already? Was she really that far gone? Almost immediately, however, the odd emotion she aroused turned to fear and anger.

"No," he rasped. "I'm never going to stop. I'm never going to stop hurting you. You're too frightened. That's what I like."

Before she could upset him anymore, he left her alone so she could use the san or rest, do whatever she wanted to get herself ready for him.

CHAPTER 8

He found, however, that his drive for her flesh had inexplicably soured. Somehow, the memory of his new roommates in the reform school made him think harder about the dangers of his present position. He was risking too much. Granted that his treatment of Morn Hyland felt as good as he said it did, it still wasn't worth the risk of remaining stationary, hidden, without repairs.

He had no way to assess absolutely the damage which had been done to his ship. Metal fatigue had strange effects. *Bright Beauty*'s bulkheads might have been weakened; they might start to leak soon—might even rupture. And Morn was *his:* he could have her anytime. Therefore it was stupid to remain where he was, risking himself to gain nothing.

While she took an interminable shower—trying, he supposed

with a leer, to get clean of his touch—he began turning some of *Bright Beauty*'s systems back on.

First, in self-defense, he programmed a new series of priority codes and alerts, circumscribing what Morn would be able to do when he gave her access to a console; he arranged warnings for himself if she tried to do anything else. When that was done, he started testing his scanners and sifters.

His tests confirmed what he already knew: *Bright Beauty* had a dangerous blind spot where her ports and antennae had been smashed. That meant he would have to run her under spin, rotating constantly so the sweep of functioning sniffers and sensors could compensate for the blindness. A problem in more ways than one: tricky for the pilot; more difficult to analyze incoming data. But there would be one advantage. While *Bright Beauty* was spinning, Morn wouldn't be able to move around: she would have to stay in her g-seat, strapped against the pull. One less detail to worry about.

He was almost ready to summon her for her first lessons when a small blip on his screen began flashing.

His heart nearly failed at the sight. Instinctive alarm poured through him, as if *Bright Beauty* were under attack. But of course she wasn't, he knew that, *knew* that, despite the way his hands shook as he keyed in commands, identified the alert.

Sickbay.

Morn Hyland was no novice. They'd taught her well in the Academy. During the few seconds he spent identifying the alert, she succeeded in reprogramming the sickbay computer.

Her instructions copied across his screen. She was telling the sickbay to give her a lethal injection of nerve-juice.

*Morn.*

Angus Thermopyle was a coward: he was at his best when he was afraid. Without thinking about it, without time to think about it, he knew that overriding the sickbay computer from his console would be too slow. There were too many steps to go through; the injection might start before he completed them. And he'd long ago eliminated the automatic safeguards from his medical equipment. Sickbay computers were programmed to preserve rather than endanger the lives of their patients—but scalpels and drugs were such convenient ways of getting rid of crew he despised that he'd deliberately deleted all restrictions from the sickbay systems.

Taking advantage of the asteroid's thin gravity, he flung himself out of his g-seat, kicked himself almost floating in the direction of the sickbay.

At the same time, he grabbed in his pocket for the zone-implant control.

He'd had a lot of practice during the past few days: he was adept at finding the right buttons on the control. Hardly more than four seconds after he understood the alert, he squeezed the function button which rendered her catatonic.

But even that took too long. She'd outsmarted him. She'd stretched out on the berth before keying in her instructions: she'd even strapped herself down. The fact that she was now as blank as a disconnected circuit couldn't save her from the cybernetic probe which reached toward her from the sickbay's equipment bank, aiming its needle for the vein in the side of her neck.

As fast as fear, Angus heaved his bulk through the doorway and grappled for the probe. Too quickly to be careful, he snatched at the needle with his fingers, snapped it off.

At once, the probe stopped. A malfunction light signaled at him from the computer panel.

He ignored it. Even though Morn was catatonic, he knotted his fists on her shoulders, shook her. *"What's the matter with you?"* he raged into her empty face. *"Are you out of your MIND?"*

The fact that she couldn't respond made his desire to hit her unbearable. But when he let go of her to brace himself, cock his arm, one of his hands left a small smudge of blood on her shoulder.

Oh, shit.

He jerked up his hand, gaped at it.

Breaking the needle had scratched his fingers.

He thought he could see a clear fluid mingling with his blood around the scratch.

Oh, *shit*. Nerve-juice was a clear fluid: colorless, tasteless, odorless; attractive only to neurons in their synapses; capable of killing.

With difficulty, he resisted a lunatic impulse to put his fingers in his mouth and suck at the wound.

Nevertheless, he knew exactly what to do. Desperation was almost normal for him.

A rapid slap-and-jerk motion unstrapped Morn from the berth. Careless of her condition, he shoved her to the floor and climbed into her place. Then he turned to the computer's control panel.

Emergency.

Cancel injection.

Clear malfunction.

Treat nerve-juice poisoning.

Source of poisoning: right hand.

Trying not to hurry, not to speed up the spread of the juice by hurrying, he stretched himself on his back and opened his right hand for the probes.

With mechanical efficiency, the probes cleaned and sealed his scratch. Attaching a new needle, the cybernetic arm gave him an injection which—according to the monitor—contained a small dose of a block that would cause the nerve-juice to be flushed out of him as waste rather than absorbed as poison.

Coincidentally, the shot also contained a significant amount of cat to ease his supercharged pulse and respiration.

The whole treatment took less than a minute.

Feeling a little light-headed, a little giddy, Angus sat up and looked at Morn Hyland's crumpled form.

She was wearing a shipsuit. Even though she intended to kill herself, she'd gotten dressed first. Maybe she could no longer bear the sight of her own body—of the physical frame which had brought the spirit inside so much grief. Despite the shipsuit, however—and despite her contorted posture, arranged for her by the force of his shove and the asteroid's g—she'd never looked so poignant to him, so lost and desirable.

Cat was having a strange effect on him. A sense of eerie calm filled him as he took the zone-implant control out of his pocket and released her.

A twitch ran through her: her eyes jerked open. For a moment she seemed unable to focus her mind on what had happened. Then she saw the way he was looking at her, and her whole face turned to despair.

"Get up," he said gruffly, but without violence.

As if what she felt were choking her, she remained where she was at first, clamped rigidly about herself and unable to move. Slowly, however, the spasm eased. She unbent her limbs, got her legs under her; finally she stood in front of him. But she refused to lift her eyes to his face.

In his mind, he saw himself hitting her. He felt his arm rise heavily, felt the shock as the back of his fist caught her face. She deserved it. But he didn't do it. His calm was amazing.

Maybe he'd accomplished something wonderful by making her desperate enough to attempt suicide.

"I want you alive," he said quietly. "If you ever try that again, I'm going to do things to you that'll make what you've already been through look romantic. Don't think there isn't anything worse. There is. If I want, I can take you to the nearest bootleg shipyard and make you a public screw for every syphilitic illegal in the whole fucking belt."

Then he shifted himself off the berth. In a state of grace, as if he'd just granted her absolution, he said, "Come on. I want you to start earning your keep," and lumbered away toward *Bright Beauty*'s command module.

He still wasn't sure why he hadn't hit her. Must have been the effect of the cat. Or of the possibility that soon she might be desperate enough to fall in love with him.

CHAPTER 9

In fact, he had every intention of taking her to the nearest bootleg shipyard. He also had every intention of castrating the first man who so much as put a finger on her. He discovered, however, he didn't have that choice.

The truth came to him two days later, while Morn was running *Bright Beauty* through a warm-up, getting ready to lift out of hiding. Morn was a fast learner—much faster than he'd expected. And one thing she'd learned was how to obey him in a way he found reassuring, a way which defused his possessive desire to keep all of *Bright Beauty* under his control.

She'd become subdued, pale in her emotions as well as in her looks. Apparently her sheer abhorrence of his lusts had broken down her resistance to him. And at the same time she was reassured, stabilized, by the fact that she now had something to do, a role which involved ships and skill. As if she were actually grateful to him for letting her work, she obeyed him so implicitly and so well that she instilled confidence. Impressed despite himself by the speed, accuracy, and compliance with which she served his ship, he went so far as to disconnect some of his waldos and relays, transferring a number of secondary functions to her console.

As soon as he did that, of course, he worried about it. But a little ingenious programming enabled him to install a parallel control for her zone implant on his board, so that he could turn her on and off without having to reach into his pocket—a reach which might not be easy in a crisis, under spin and g.

Calm once again, he actually stopped watching what she did and let her get *Bright Beauty* ready for lift-off by herself. While she worked on that, he spent some time analyzing his finances.

Then he spent more time cursing savagely to himself—all the more savagely because he didn't want her to hear him, so he had to keep his mouth shut.

Money was why he couldn't go where he'd intended. No matter how well they knew him—maybe because of how well they knew him—the shipyard just inside forbidden space wouldn't so much as cycle their airlocks for him on spec. Even their hunger for the goods he supplied, the goods they fenced for him, wouldn't inspire them to extend credit. If he were unable to pay in advance for the work *Bright Beauty* needed, the work wouldn't be done. And if he tried to run a bluff, he risked murder or worse; risked having his ship snatched from him.

Of course, repairs were cheaper on Com-Mine Station. And some people were even given credit. But that was out of the question. In order for the Station shipyard to do repairs, the workmen would need access to some of his ship's secrets. And they would never keep what they discovered to themselves: he was sure of that. They would talk; and Security would hear about it; and he might never get out of dock again.

He couldn't get *Bright Beauty* fixed until he had more money.

He chewed on that for a while, until the implications made him feel cornered and murderous—more like his old self than he had felt for days. Then he snapped at Morn, "Shut down."

He appreciated the way she obeyed, without hesitation; so he glared at her like a butcher of babies as she quickly and precisely reversed the warm-up, settled *Bright Beauty* to cool, and keyed off her console before turning to face him.

"I'm sorry," she said dully. "What did I do wrong?"

Her assumption that she'd made a mistake pleased him, despite his anger. He dismissed it with a snarl. Brutally, trying to startle the truth out of her because for some reason he was reluctant to trust anything she might tell him under the influence of her zone implant, he demanded, "How many people back on Com-Mine know you're after me?"

She was startled; he saw that. Several different responses flickered like hints across her face before she spoke.

"We weren't after you."

"You found me, didn't you?" he rasped. For some reason, it frightened him to realize he was going to believe whatever she told him. "You can't expect me to think you were looking for those pissed-out miners. Captain Davies fucking Hyland knew my name. Of course you were after me."

"Yes." She spoke slowly, as if she had trouble remembering that part of her past. "Sort of. We didn't know anything about you when we came out from Earth. I mean personally. But Com-Mine Security gave us your name. Just a list of 'suspicious characters'— people to watch out for, ships. They didn't do that because we're UMCP. They didn't know. It's standard procedure for them—they give the same list to any legitimate oreliner that asks. And a lot of rumors mentioned you. We correlated that with the way you pulled out so soon after we arrived. Almost like you knew who we were. That made us interested in you. Very interested. How did you know who we were?

"But we weren't *after* you specifically. We were on patrol, that's all. Looking for pirates. Mine jumpers. Bootleg operations. We just happened to find you."

The effort of memory hurt her: she had to reach back through so much horror. Therefore she was telling the truth.

" 'Just happened,' " he snorted. "Don't try to con me, bitch. I was in a played-out part of the belt. The only people there who need *protecting* are scavengers. Like those miners. You don't patrol places like that. You patrol where the money is."

Again her expression hinted at horror. She'd killed her whole family. "You forget. We were covert—pretending to be a new oreliner. If we wanted to lure anybody after us, we had to go some-where unexpected—somewhere that would surprise people who knew the belt.

"That's the main thing we were trying to do. Lure somebody like you to follow us.

"But I suppose we *were* after you, in a way. Even if we weren't covert, it's standard practice for ships like *Starmaster* to go where they aren't expected. Shake people up a little. And the way you headed out when we came in made us think you were ripe for shaking. We didn't know where to find you, but we thought it made sense to scan the nearest played-out parts of the belt first, just to see what we could stir up. Where would a ship go if she wanted to hide?

"I guess it was a deliberate coincidence. It happened because we were trying to make it happen. We were looking for you. But we weren't doing anything out of the ordinary." She spoke tonelessly, without expression, holding herself numb to pain. "Until you blasted those miners, we knew there was always the chance you were innocent."

"All right. All *right*." His glare was yellow with malice and fear, but he didn't get out of his g-seat, or make her come to him, or work any of the buttons on her zone-implant control. "If you fuckers left me alone, none of this would have happened. You haven't answered my question. Who did you tell? Who knew what you were doing?"

For a moment or two she remained silent, staring at her board. Then she sighed. "Nobody. That's the whole point of going covert. When we come out from Earth, we don't know who we can trust. So we don't tell anybody anything. We do our job and take the rest one step at a time.

"The last mission my fa—Captain Hyland was on, somebody in Station Center turned out to be feeding information to half a dozen pirates. It's better if we don't tell anybody anything."

Angus believed her. In fact, the only reason he'd doubted her at all was that the intensity of his need to believe her made him suspicious. Everything hinged on it. At the moment, he had no other hope. He couldn't run *Bright Beauty* in this condition indefinitely. Sooner or later, she would fail him if he put that much pressure on her.

But if Morn were telling the truth—

If she were telling the truth, he could get away with it. It might be the riskiest bluff he'd tried in years, but he could get away with it.

If she were telling the truth.

And if he could control her.

If he could break her into small enough pieces.

Abruptly he heaved himself out of his g-seat. "Come on." Ignoring the involuntary revulsion that ached across her features before she could suppress it, he headed toward the sickbay. "You kept your mouth shut for the cops. I'm going to make sure you do the same for me."

In the sickbay he studied her face, drilled her, dredged the information he needed out of her, and drove himself between her legs in spasms of fear and hope. Eagerly, avidly, he watched her for signs that she was falling in love—that she was growing dependent on her helplessness.

# CHAPTER 10

He did his best to believe it was happening. In an odd way, as long as he kept her alive his survival depended on her: he could be truly safe only if he killed her and disposed of her body. And that option was one he no longer considered. He was as likely to destroy *Bright Beauty* as to murder Morn. Therefore he couldn't afford to be wrong. He had to break her and be sure of it; damage her so much that he could trust the results.

Because he was afraid, he was in no danger of trusting them prematurely.

In the end, however, his success was inevitable. After all, what choice did she have? He'd made himself her entire world; he was everything she felt. He knew how this kind of pressure worked: it had been tried on him more than once. His control of her circumstances—as well as of her physical being—was absolute. With the tap of a button, he could reduce her mind to a brute howl of pain. When she satisfied him, he could reward her, not with pleasure— for some reason, he was reluctant to see what she would look like pleased—but with relief from hurt; with sleep; with the occasional opportunity to choose her own movements, take care of herself in her own way.

By degrees, he beat her down until she was like a child toward him: dependent; urgent to please. He taught her that his survival was hers as well; that any peril he met would hit her first, and harder. And he played on the bizarre ethic to which she'd sworn herself when she became a cop. Again and again, he assured her that she deserved what was happening to her. She'd killed her family, hadn't she? She'd betrayed them all. No, it wasn't something she'd done by conscious choice. It was worse: it was something she'd done because of who she was; because of the fundamental flaw which left her vulnerable to gap-sickness.

With all his cunning, he worked to deprive her of her capacity to think in any terms which didn't come to her from him.

And he watched the results, studied them with a coward's intuitive precision. He saw the darkness accumulating in her gaze; the gradual slackening of her skin; the change in the way she moved, so that every action became a limp. When he fucked her, he felt her begin to respond, driven to swallow her revulsion by self-loathing and the need to satisfy him. When she slept, he heard her whimpering for help which never came.

At last even his grubby, suspicious nature believed that she'd been damaged enough to risk.

Still cautious, he prepared his safeguards and coercions. Then, with a UMC cop for crew, he took his ship out of hiding.

Six days later, *Bright Beauty* sputtered into Com-Mine Station's control space and requested permission to dock.

No one asked any awkward questions at that point. No one had reason to: no one knew *Starmaster* was lost. *Bright Beauty* was given permission to dock and instructed to await normal inspection.

The inspector assigned to clear Angus Thermopyle and *Bright Beauty* wasn't particularly interested in his job that day. Even brain-numb on cat, however, he could hardly have failed to notice the anomalous fact that Angus had left Com-Mine Station purportedly alone and now returned with a woman as crew.

He didn't ask Angus to explain this detail. He had no wish to risk making a fool of himself. Instead, he got Morn's name and fed it into the Station's id computer.

After that, the situation got messy.

*Bright Beauty* was slapped in quarantine, and a whole parade of inspectors trooped through her, asking questions, issuing directives, making demands. As the inspectors went up in rank—therefore in determination to be obeyed—their questions and directives and demands became more aggressive and personal. And all of them were aimed at Morn Hyland.

What happened to *Starmaster*?

How did you survive?

How did you end up with *him*?

Unfortunately, the authorities found themselves in a frustrating position. Center was worried—in fact, outright alarmed—about *Starmaster*. Security practically salivated for the chance to get their hands on Angus. But they had nothing to go on: no formal record of the truth about *Starmaster;* nothing but hints. And Morn refused to answer their questions. She was a cop—and she refused.

Periodically, an inspector tried to appropriate *Bright Beauty*'s datacore. Angus positively declined to release it until he was required to do so by law—until he was formally charged with a crime.

Periodically, attempts were made to get Morn away from him. Each time, she brandished her UMCP id tag and dismissed any superior authority. Although she chose not to speak, she tacitly covered Angus with her police mantle.

The more perceptive Station personnel observed that there was more than a little pain in the way she stood beside Angus. For a cop, she looked unusually vulnerable; almost frightened. If they'd met her alone in the halls of DelSec, they would have assumed she was a derelict. If they were kind, they would have tried to help her.

But here they could do nothing. Her id tag put her beyond challenge. And Angus held his ground with his hands in the pockets of his shipsuit, glowering at everybody and stonewalling expertly.

What happened to *Starmaster*?

Blew up, he answered for her. For no reason. Must have been sabotage. We'll give you the coordinates if you want to search the wreck.

How did you survive?

Freak accident. The auxiliary bridge held. She still would have died eventually, but I rescued her.

Angus could see the terrible hurt behind her eyes, but he relied on the zone implant to keep her quiet. And he relied on her silence—and her id tag—to baffle the inspectors.

Why are you with him? He's a known pirate. We just haven't been able to prove it yet. You're UMCP. What kind of hold has he got on you? Do you actually expect us to believe he's telling the *truth*?

I don't care what you believe, Angus said with relish. I told you. *Starmaster* blew up. She was sabotaged. That must have been done here. Before she left Com-Mine Station. Morn nodded dully. Angus glowered at everybody and kept his hand in his pocket. She doesn't know who she can trust, but she's damn sure she can't trust *you*.

The inspectors wheedled and demanded, but they were unable to make Morn speak.

The only question they really wanted Angus to answer was: What happened to your ship? You look like you've been in a dog-fight.

Look again. Scan me. That isn't matter fire. I got hit by a rock.

An experienced "captain" like you? That must have been some rock.

I was in the belt. I was running *Bright Beauty* by myself. I miscalculated. Is that a crime?

The inspectors were in no mood to give up, however. They tried to trap him.

*Starmaster* was after you. You crashed trying to run. Isn't that the truth?

No.

Then how did you happen to be the one who came to the rescue—you with a damaged ship?

Coincidence. I was close enough. The blast made my scan go crazy. Radio interference. Particle noise. That kind of static doesn't happen unless there's been a disaster, so I tracked it back and found her. With an effort, Angus refrained from pointing out how virtuous his conduct had been.

The dock manifest says you left without buying supplies. Your air scrubbers should have failed a long time ago. How come you're still breathing?

Rescuer's privilege. I took filters from her ship.

His bluff was working. As long as Morn didn't come apart under the strain, he was going to be safe.

Why is she staying with you? What's your hold on her?

She's going to hire somebody to carry a message back to Earth. We'd do it ourselves, but *Bright Beauty* can't cross the gap. When UMCPHQ sends out instructions, she'll know what to do. Until then, she trusts me more than you.

In the end, the inspectors had no choice. Of course, they didn't believe the story. Under other circumstances, they might have stretched the law far enough to keep *Bright Beauty* quarantined at least until Station techs had a chance to visit and analyze *Starmaster*'s wreckage. But Morn Hyland was UMCP; not under Station jurisdiction. The assumption had to be made that she knew what she was doing, that her actions were reasonable and shouldn't be interfered with.

*Bright Beauty* was cleared.

Angus Thermopyle took Morn Hyland directly to DelSec.

His bluff had worked.

He had no actual desire to go to Mallorys. He wanted to seal his hatches and fuck Morn until she wept. It was still possible that his hold on her might snap, and he didn't want to risk her in public. But he knew he was going to be watched for a long time—at least until inspectors got back from *Starmaster*. It was important to behave normally. At that moment, "normal" meant Mallorys, where he could start trying to buy the information he needed to make money.

He'd been walking down the path to his doom for some time. Now his doom started moving toward him.

Even though she was unfamiliar with DelSec, he stayed half a step behind Morn's shoulder so he could keep an eye on her. At once elated and afraid, possessive and angry, he noticed how every man they passed looked at her—noticed it and hated them. In the same way that he'd planned revenge against *Starmaster* for driving him off Com-Mine Station, he now evolved elaborate, impossible schemes which would teach all these bastards to fear him. It was conceivable that he could claim salvage on *Starmaster*. Morn's UMCP id tag might make that possible. With enough money, he would get *Bright Beauty* rebuilt, better than before. Then he would be invulnerable. He could do anything he wanted.

Dreams like that helped him endure the crowds he despised in DelSec and Mallorys.

He hated Mallorys, of course. But it was better than any of the alternatives. As a group, the drunks and ruins and illegals there knew more and cared less than the rest of the people in DelSec. They meant him harm in ways he understood. For that reason, they were less dangerous than they thought.

Station gravity—roughly .9g—made him feel leaden, bloated; he was in no mood for a drink. His bluff had worked! But everybody on Com-Mine was waiting for him to make a mistake and get caught; all the inspectors, everybody in Security, every prospector or miner who'd ever tried the belt, everybody in Mallorys who knew his reputation and didn't trust him. And Morn walked as if the weight meant nothing—as if in spite of the many ways it could be hurt, her body carried its beauty easily. All those men wanted her. They wanted to get her away from him.

He was already feeling frightened and bloodthirsty when he caught sight of Nick Succorso through the heat and din of Mallorys.

At once, he felt like he'd been hit in the chest by an impact-ram—more so because he couldn't show it, didn't dare react in front of all these people, let them see his weakness.

He would have recognized Nick as an enemy immediately in any case: he knew how to interpret that careless grin, that sharp, buccaneering gleam of humor and superiority. He knew Nick's contempt for him was instantaneous. He was ugly and luckless and not very clean, and Nick had already begun to sneer at him.

Under any circumstances, Angus would have gone a long way out of his way to damage Nick Succorso. That was instinctive and fundamental, like his initial panic when he saw *Starmaster*.

But this was worse, much worse: this was like watching someone aim a rifle straight into his face and fire. He saw Nick glance at him, dismiss him—and look at Morn. He saw the scars that underlined Nick's gaze darken, as if his vision had begun to smolder. And he saw Morn's reaction.

Her face betrayed nothing. She said nothing. But he knew her intimately—knew every pulse of her heartbeat, every hue of her skin, every shade of horror and hurt in the depths of her eyes. He knew immediately, in front of all those people, without another second for consideration or effort, that Nick Succorso had more power over her than he did.

Nick had the power to make her want him.

And yet that recognition was only the beginning: the full truth was still worse. Until this moment, when he saw and understood— or thought he understood—the way Morn and Nick looked at each other, Angus Thermopyle hadn't known how weak he really was. He hadn't realized how much power he lacked—and how much he wanted that power, how much he grieved for it. He could make— had made—Morn do anything and everything his lust or loathing conceived. Like a drunk or a derelict, he'd believed that was enough.

But it wasn't enough, oh no, never enough, not now. He'd duped himself, blinded and fooled himself.

He'd taught her to cooperate in her own degradation. He'd taught her to act as if he were necessary to her. No matter what he did, however, he could never make her *want* him. The buttons on the zone implant control which tuned her so that every nerve in her body obeyed his desire were impotent compared to the jaunty burn of Nick's gaze.

It wasn't fair. She belonged to Angus. She was *his*.

He had no way to know he was wrong.

CHAPTER 11

The truth was that Morn Hyland didn't see Nick Succorso as a sexual being at all. On that point, everyone who noticed her situation or gave any thought to her reactions was wrong. She hardly noticed Nick was male. If she had, she would have turned her back on him, would have refused him with the same debased instinct for survival which had caused her to refuse any possibility of hope which the Station inspectors might have represented.

She didn't want a man. Any male touch would have made her ache to scream and puke, just as Angus himself did: She'd been raped and raped until the violation had reached through her flesh to her spirit; pain and abhorrence had soaked into the marrow of her bones. If Nick Succorso had put his hand on her as a man, she would have flinched away, exactly as she did when Angus touched her.

Angus had more power over her than he realized.

Yet he was right when he sensed that something leapt up inside Morn at the sight of Nick Succorso.

That "something," however, had nothing whatever to do with Nick's handsomeness, his virility, his physical appeal. Instead it had to do with his look of raffish eagerness, his scarred and buccaneering appearance of bravado. She wanted him, not as a man, but as an effective force. He might be strong and cunning—not to mention unscrupulous—enough to destroy the man who was destroying her.

Did she think Nick might set her free, redeem her from her anguish? No. Angus had come too close to breaking her. She no longer had the imagination—or the courage—to dream so far.

But he'd taught her how to hate. And she had learned that lesson profoundly. Her own hate lived with the pain and abhorrence in the marrow of her bones. The "something" which had leapt up in her at the sight of Nick Succorso was simply the hope that Angus could be beaten.

As for Nick himself—

Like Angus, the other people in Mallorys were wrong about him as well.

Oh, he noticed her beauty immediately and was attracted to it. His virility was no sham: his taste for lovely female flesh never left him. In part for that reason, he had nurtured a wide reputation as a lover. But he had other reasons also. He liked winning, so he did whatever was necessary to make his women respond to him passionately. And he had a hunger for revenge; especially sexual revenge. He yearned to get even.

The truth—which he kept to himself—was that he didn't actually like women. In secret, he feared and despised them. Their bodies had value only to the extent that his response to them could draw an even greater response from them. Where such satisfactions weren't at issue, he had no interest in them. He preferred seeing them hurt.

The explanation for this was a mystery only in the sense that he never spoke of it.

Once, when he was barely a man in years, and no more than a boy in experience, he'd been bested by a woman. And as she beat him, cheated him, ruined his dreams, she sneered at him. His scars were the marks of her contempt, the visible sign that she hadn't considered him worth killing. Everyone else she *had* killed, every other man on that ship, nearly twenty of them; but him she'd left with only his scars to remember her by. There was nothing he could do that would make her fear him.

That ship had been the original *Captain's Fancy,* the inspiration of the name Nick now used for his pretty frigate. The love he felt for his present ship was an echo of his yearning for that earlier vessel. She'd been his dream from the moment when he'd first become old enough to have such dreams.

Nick Succorso—which, incidentally, wasn't his real name—had been born station-bound in the same sense that some people were planet-bound, unable or unwilling to leave for one reason or another. He was the son of a family of administrators living on a station like Com-Mine, but half a hundred parsecs away, a station that tended one of the official (therefore rich) trading routes between Earth and forbidden space. There he'd begun watching scan at an early age, just as most of the children of administrators did on that station, to learn the skills they would need for the rest of their lives.

Unlike most of his peers, however, he'd fallen in love with what he watched, with the vast gulf of space and the lure of the gap, with the romance of sailing the imponderable stellar winds, with the mysterious lurch-and-translation which took men and ships across dimensions beyond the reach of their former lives.

Specifically, he'd fallen in love with *Captain's Fancy*.

She seemed to him the bravest of the best, a trim metal sheath of power which pierced the heavens and the gap. Her lines were sleek, yet she bristled with weapons. Her holds were huge, yet she swept across scan and docked and undocked as gracefully as a creature of the great deep. Her crew were exotic men drawn from the strangest parts of the galaxy, men with the strength to pit themselves against the vacuum and forbidden space, and the wealth they traded was fabulous. Young Nick Succorso ached to sign aboard their ship under any imaginable contract or conditions.

Good heavens, no! said his mother.

Are you out of your mind? asked his father.

As for the captain of *Captain's Fancy*, he simply said, No. Regal as a lord in his braid and authority, he dismissed Nick out of hand. If the command second hadn't taken pity on Nick's crushed look, Nick never would have been given any explanation at all. But the command second, who meant well, had taken the time to say, Forget it, kid. We never take crew from stationers. Too much trouble. Haven't got the instincts. Only way you'll ever get on a ship is, go to one of the academies. Earth. Aleph Green. Orion's Reach.

Good heavens, no! his mother repeated.

Are you out of your mind? demanded his father. What makes you think we've got that kind of money?

Nick was never stupid. He could see his dreams curdling. He would never be able to earn "that kind of money" by himself. The only jobs which paid that well were jobs on ships.

But he couldn't bear to see his dreams curdle, so he let something else inside him go sour.

He began to plot crimes.

In those days, piracy was a constant and maddening problem across the shipping lanes. The UMC Police were relatively new;

their ability to enforce the laws Earth made didn't reach far. And forbidden space didn't appear to make any reliable distinction between sanctioned and dishonest trade.

With the logic of the young, Nick reasoned that wherever there was piracy, there were pirates. And wherever there were pirates, there was a demand for information.

Destinations. Cargoes. Arrival dates. Departure trajectories. Route clearances.

Nick worked scan. Indirectly, at least, he had access to that kind of information.

Even as a youth, hardly a young man yet, he was someone whose chances came to him when he needed them, when he was ready for them. As soon as he was sour enough, and had made his plans sufficiently concrete, and had developed his access to information, he met the woman who scarred him.

The scars came later, of course. She knew what she was doing and did it well. First came casual conversation. Casual drinks. Casual sex. His first casual mention of *Captain's Fancy* passed as if she hadn't heard it. Only after he'd told her enough about his plans, his information, his needs—only then did she let him see the hunger in her eyes.

She wanted that ship.

And he was really just a kid. He didn't have any trouble convincing himself that she wanted *Captain's Fancy* the same way he did.

So he betrayed the ship he loved. He thought he would end up as part of her new crew. Eventually—so the dream went—he would end up as her new captain.

For what he later swore was the last time in his life, he was wrong.

The woman took him with her aboard her own ship. He was

with her as she ambushed *Captain's Fancy,* crippled the merchanter, forced the vessel to surrender. He accompanied her when she boarded the drifting hulk.

Already reality diverged from his dream. *Captain's Fancy* wasn't supposed to be ruined like this. As for the regal captain and his crew—Nick wanted them humiliated, of course; but he was a bit young to stomach such frank slaughter.

Nevertheless reality continued to diverge.

The woman didn't take him with her when she left. After killing the crew, emptying the holds, gutting the communication gear, she laughed at Nick and scarred him and abandoned him.

He pleaded, of course. He believed he loved her. He believed she loved him. He was young enough to have persuaded himself of almost anything for the sake of his dreams. But his ideas of love only made her giggle in scorn. Her knife told him what she thought of having him in her bed. When she left, there were tears streaming through the blood into his mouth.

After that, he was alone on a wreck a million kilometers from the station, with no skills, no knowledge—and no engines. By rights, he should have died.

He didn't. Instead, he became the Nick Succorso he was now. By the time he'd contrived to be rescued—some rather ingenious manipulation of *Captain's Fancy's* residual emissions produced the effect of a beacon and eventually attracted a passing cruiser—he'd assumed the id files and certifications of the ship's cabin boy, the real Nick Succorso, and had taught himself the skills to back up his new credentials.

Once rescued, of course, he'd given the UMCP everything he knew about the woman who cut him. That enabled them to harry her out of his part of space. He never saw her again.

Naturally, however, he never forgot her. From the time of his first legitimate shipboard post until the day when he snatched the present *Captain's Fancy* for himself, from the moment of his first successful raid until now, she was always with him. His scars grew dark under his eyes whenever he saw something he wanted, something that wasn't his; the slashes on his cheeks turned the color of curdled blood.

Under other circumstances, he wouldn't have lifted a finger to help Morn Hyland. Women in pain were the next best thing to women who loved him. Both pain and love helped him get even.

But under *these* circumstances—

Nick Succorso was drawn to the idea of rescuing Morn for several reasons. Angus Thermopyle himself was one of them. Nick knew Angus' reputation, of course: he knew Angus wasn't just a competitor; he was a dangerous competitor. And Nick was prepared to tolerate competition only as long as it wasn't good enough—wasn't dangerous enough—to get in his way; to cast him in the shade. He saw Morn Hyland immediately as a handle on Angus, a lever to use against the competition.

His other reasons were more complex.

Her relevance—if any—to his concerns as the master of *Captain's Fancy* was unclear. Did he see her as a source of wealth? Did he mean to exact ransom from the Hyland family? From Com-Mine Station? The UMCP itself? He may have had a source of information about her that wasn't generally available. If so, he didn't mention it.

However, her relevance to his personal buccaneering was plain enough.

In some of its details, her condition was obvious at a glance. She was attached to a man she hated, fixed to an illegal who repelled her. What did that imply about her? On this point, his reasoning was unique in Mallorys. For him, her attachment implied, not that she was subject to coercion, but that her capacity to respond was so intense, so overwhelming, that she couldn't control it. She couldn't help herself.

And if she had *that* kind of response to someone like Angus Thermopyle, if her own passions left her *that* abject—

Nick Succorso's scars darkened and his mouth actually went dry at the thought of how Morn's passions might make her respond to him.

So Angus Thermopyle was wrong about Nick—as wrong as he was about Morn herself. But he was also right. The danger was real. Without a word to each other, with no more contact between them than a gaze or two, they had banded together against him.

And he had to face it all, realize it all, and swallow it, show nothing. Instinct was of no use to him here. He was cornered by his situation, trapped with a perception he would have cheerfully committed murder to avoid. He needed money. Therefore he needed Mallorys; needed the people who came to Mallorys and sold secrets. In addition, Security was watching him. Even in DelSec, there were spies. He was being studied for any sign of a mistake, scrutinized for any evidence of weakness. He couldn't afford to give himself away by retreating; by revealing that he recognized his danger.

He stayed where he was, keeping his mask of belligerent disinterest in place, simply because he was afraid of the consequences if he did anything else.

Gruffly he ordered Morn to a seat at one of the condensation-stained tables—a seat with her back to Nick Succorso. He made sure the way he talked to her was loud enough to be overheard, so her obedience would be noticed. Then he sat down beside her and squeezed her against him possessively. Look at us, you bastards, you motherfucking sons of shit. Look at her. She's *mine*. Mine!

He put on a good performance. Nobody in Mallorys knew that

he'd witnessed the way Morn and Nick looked at each other, that
he'd felt the electricity between them. But his success gave him no
satisfaction. It was Morn he wanted, her desire, her willingness—
the parts of herself which he'd been unable to extort from her; the
parts which she'd just given away.

He was going to have to kill Nick. There was no other answer.
There was no other way to hurt her enough, to punish her for doing
this to him.

Through a haze of rage and grief, he ordered drinks he didn't
want and paid for them. He heard people talking around him. Some
of them spoke to him. He spoke to some of them. The ones who
mattered knew why he was here, what he wanted; he didn't need
to go looking for them, not yet.

By no flicker of attention or shift of expression did Morn betray
she knew Nick Succorso was alive. But Angus read the heightened
hue of her skin and thought he understood it.

Through sheer force of panic, he stayed in Mallorys for more
than an hour: long enough to appear normal; to ensure the word
would be passed that Angus Thermopyle was back on station; long
enough so no one would guess he was afraid. Then he took Morn
back to *Bright Beauty*.

She expected trouble. He saw it in the covert way she glanced
at him, in the concealed alarm and compliance of her posture. She
had a secret now, an intention she needed to protect. Well, good
for her. He meant trouble. He was perfectly willing to defile and
humiliate every inch of her to take the sting out of his heart. His
stomach was a knot of black hate, and his brain was so full of violence
he could hardly keep his balance.

When they'd boarded the ship, he made a deliberate and me-
ticulous show of sealing the hatches, rigging security alarms, cutting
off communication; isolating *Bright Beauty* from the Station, as if

he wanted to prolong the suspense for her, give her every chance to be terrified by what was coming.

After that, he engaged her zone-implant control.

He planned only to make her passive. He wanted her to see and feel everything he did. But his fingers seemed to have a mind of their own. His whole body ignored the dark ruin clamoring inside him. Instead of tuning Morn to passivity, or even catatonia, he pushed the buttons which put her to sleep. Then he scooped her up in his arms and carried her to a berth.

He settled her on the thin mattress; adjusted a pillow under her head; tucked a blanket around her, securing it to its g-seals. While his stomach clenched and tore, and his brain reeled, he left her and closed off the passageway to her cabin, locking himself alone in the command module.

Then he started to howl like a grief-stricken beast.

# CHAPTER 12

He would have been better off if he had gone to a bootleg ship-yard, of course. Perhaps he could have sold Morn's favors for the money he needed to get *Bright Beauty* made whole. Power over her would have brought a much higher price there than on Com-Mine Station. And—assuming Nick Succorso followed him—he could have faced his enemy in a more naked and therefore fairer arena.

He would have been better off if he'd simply undocked from Com-Mine Station, launched a few torpedoes at *Captain's Fancy*, and then fled for his life.

He would have been better off if he'd killed Morn Hyland and ashed her in *Bright Beauty*'s thruster tubes.

In fact, from moment to moment during the next two standard weeks he fully intended to do any one or all of those things. But he didn't.

Instead, he worked on arranging Nick's destruction.

First, of course, he took care of *Bright Beauty*. He had her serviced as thoroughly as possible without major repairs. He paid for X-ray analysis to test her shell and bulkheads for metal fatigue. He bought all the new components he could afford. And he gave her name and id letters a fresh coat of paint.

At the same time, however, he asked questions whenever he could. He paid sums which nearly broke him for information—even for hints. And finally, guided by those hints, for one brief, glorious moment he succeeded at breaking into the Station's main computer. Before the computer's security systems forced him to retreat so that his intrusion wouldn't be traced, he pulled as much data as he could.

By some standards, it wasn't much. Routine files aside, all he gleaned was the codes and routing by which *Captain's Fancy* talked to the Station's computer network.

In theory, this knowledge was useless to him. After all, he couldn't get at the physical lines which carried *Captain's Fancy*'s business to the computers and back again. Anything that tampered with the integrity of those lines would register immediately. And knowledge of the codes and routing was pointless without access to the actual data-stream.

Angus was desperate, however. In his own opinion, he'd lost his mind. In self-defense, he put Morn to sleep, so that she wouldn't know about and couldn't interfere with what he did. Then, hyperventilating so hard that his suit could hardly keep up with it, and sweating like a beast, he went EVA.

He got away with it because it was such an odd thing to do. People who wanted to work outside their ships did so in the shipyard, over on the other side of Com-Mine. And only men as suspicious as Angus himself scanned the ships around them while they were in dock. Apparently Nick Succorso wasn't that suspicious. Or maybe he had too much confidence in his own invulnerability. Nobody noticed what Angus was doing.

Clamped to the metal surface with limpets, and keeping his head turned grimly away from the fathomless starfield, he moved along the staggering curve of Com-Mine's skin from *Bright Beauty* to *Captain's Fancy*. When he got there, he used a current sensor to read each of the lines connecting the ship to the Station until he identified the one that carried the data-stream. Then, with savage care, he wrapped a dummy line tightly around it from output to receptacle and ran the dummy back to his ship.

Aboard *Bright Beauty* again, he didn't give himself time to recover from the ordeal of EVA. He was obsessed. His hands shook in eagerness and fear as he sent power down his line, surrounding *Captain's Fancy*'s data-stream with a delicate magnetic field. Then he put a scope on his line and watched the field for fluctuations.

It worked. Under full boost, his scope began to show a swift series of spikes and scoops, a fluttering progression too quick for the eye to interpret.

His computer had the codes and routing: now it had an echo of the actual data-stream. Soon he could call up a display of everything *Captain's Fancy* and Com-Mine Station said to each other.

Under different circumstances, his interest in this information would have been specific and temporary. He would have used what he knew to plunder Nick's finances, transfer to himself everything Nick owned. It wouldn't have been difficult to make that kind of computer transaction untraceable, using his own codes and routing. Then he would have detached his dummy line and sat back, daring anyone aboard *Captain's Fancy* to guess what had happened.

Now, however, Angus had other plans.

In a sense, the situation was simplified by the fact that Nick didn't have enough money to repair *Bright Beauty*. Despite his successful air, he was no wealthier than Angus. Without that temptation, Angus had an easier time stifling the impulse to touch or alter anything he found. He didn't want to warn his enemy of the danger, didn't want to let Nick know he was being stalked.

Instead of tampering with the data-stream, he programmed his computer to alert him if any one of a long list of key words and names appeared in the ship-Station dialogue. As an afterthought, because he was inherently suspicious, he told the computer to do the same if any unidentifiable codes were used.

Then he left *Bright Beauty* and went about the business of behaving normally.

When he returned to his ship and reviewed what his computer had gleaned, he found no mention of himself or Morn or anything he could recognize. He learned only that Nick Succorso was faithful about logging in and out of *Captain's Fancy*.

And Nick had received two messages in a code Angus' computer didn't recognize and couldn't crack.

Angus had no way to read those messages. But he could trace them because he already knew the routing.

They came from Station Security.

When he discovered that, he wanted to laugh and scream and break something and celebrate all at once. It was the perfect touch—the final reason why his bluff had worked. There was in fact a leak in Security, a traitor. Why else would Nick Succorso be receiving coded messages from that source? The vacuum-based accusation Angus had prepared to protect his hold on Morn had hit Com-Mine's inspectors where they lived: its blind accuracy had given it an almost prescient credibility.

And Nick Succorso's swashbuckling success was based on inside information. He had an ally in Security; a friend in power.

Characteristically, Angus didn't worry about *why*. He didn't even care about *how*. The fact itself was all that interested him.

Nick Succorso had an ally in Security.

That made him more dangerous. But it also diminished him. He didn't stand on his own: he was a good face with nothing behind it; empty bravado. A nerve-juice addict could do everything he did— as long as the junkie had inside information to back him up, a friend in power. Nick could sneer at anybody he wanted; but it only mattered because he had Security on his side.

"You bastard," Angus muttered through his teeth. "You shit-eating bastard. I'm going to rip your balls off."

It was just a question of when and where.

# CHAPTER 13

During this period—nearly a week—Morn Hyland spent most of her time either catatonic or asleep. When Angus wanted to use her, he did so without rousing her from the influence of her zone implant. He didn't want her to know what he was doing: he couldn't take the risk that she might find some way to sabotage him. For that reason, he got her out of bed only for meals, or to go to Mallorys with him.

Every time he used her body, he hardened his resolve against Nick Succorso. And every time he took her out in public, the desire to protect her burned as brightly as terror in him.

But the second week was different. Now Angus timed his trips away from *Bright Beauty* to coincide with Nick's absences from *Captain's Fancy*. And he wore under his shipsuit a nerve beeper, a small electrode taped to the skin and set to tingle whenever *Captain's*

*Fancy* relayed a summons for Nick through Com-Mine communications, requesting his return to his ship. Taking Morn with him now to Mallorys was part of Angus' plan, part of the bait. He wanted to make Nick see her and do something: he wanted to make Nick want her badly enough to take action.

In fact, he almost went so far as to buy her new clothes. She could be ravishing, if he gave her the chance. And he ached to do that, for his own sake as well as hers, so that she would be ravishing and *his,* like *Bright Beauty* with fresh paint.

But in the end he decided to keep her in her rumpled, ill-fitting shipsuit, not because of the money, but because of the danger. If she looked too good, she might attract trouble he wasn't ready for. And there was always the possibility—he took it seriously only because he was too suspicious to do anything else—that Nick was smart enough to smell a trap when it was smothered in perfume.

He wanted Nick to do something because almost anything he did would give Angus an excuse to kill him—and would provide as well a plea of self-defense against any murder charge. Angus could be ready for almost anything because he knew more about Nick's business and activities than Nick could guess.

And when Nick was gone, Angus would be in an ideal position to make use of what he knew about Station Security. Nick's ally might become his. A little leverage, a little blackmail, might make it possible for Angus to live as well as Nick did now.

So he made sure Nick saw Morn as often as possible. Secretly, cunningly, so that no one grasped what he was doing, he flaunted her in front of Nick, urging him, goading him.

At the same time, darkness swirled around in Angus' head and his hands itched for blood because he knew that behind her blank expression, her wounded and necessary emptiness, Morn was on fire for his enemy.

Each time he put her where she and Nick could see each other, he swore to himself, *promised,* that as soon as he got her back to the ship he was going to rip out her female organs and feed them down the garbage processor, so that no man would ever have any reason to desire her again.

And each time, when they returned to *Bright Beauty,* he couldn't control the gentleness which came over him. He flung obscenities at her with his mouth; but his touch was soft, nearly tentative. The things he made her do were strangely decorous, almost considerate, as if after depriving her of will and hope and humanity he wished her to forgive him.

She tried to hide it, but she couldn't conceal her perplexity. He knew her too well: he could read the color of her eyes, the small muscles in her cheeks. She felt the change in him, the distress, and didn't know what it meant.

Gentleness? From Angus Thermopyle? She knew *him* too well.

She watched him as if she could see that he was doomed.

Was she gloating? He believed she was. He believed that she already counted on Nick Succorso to rescue her and destroy him. He believed that she was already measuring out his blood in drops of pain. The thought made all his limbs knot with the force of his need to tear her apart.

Yet he didn't hurt her. She was too precious. And too perplexed. Her confusion had implications he couldn't begin to understand. He wasn't the kind of man who could imagine that she might be reconsidering her hate. He could never have understood that his fear and gentleness might have touched her in the very place which his abuse had made vulnerable.

Alone in the command module, he had to grind his teeth to keep from howling.

*Damn you completely to hell and horror! What have you done to me?*

He told himself he was ready. He'd been a match for men like Nick Succorso since he was twelve. And he knew everything he needed about Nick except the content of those coded messages. He was *ready*. Of course he was ready.

But the clenched ache deep down in his gut told him he wasn't ready. He felt that he was never going to be ready again.

*What have you* done *to me?*

He spent all the time his enemy allowed him feverishly trying to break that secret code. But whenever Nick left *Captain's Fancy,* Angus also took Morn out of *Bright Beauty* so that no one would know—so that he himself wouldn't know—how fundamental and compulsory his fear had become.

Finally he reached the end of his endurance. He'd waited and plotted and struggled for a week, and still Nick did nothing. Angus never doubted that some harm was being planned against him: he simply couldn't bear the suspense any longer. Any day now, he was going to fall on his knees and beg Morn to pardon him. And if that happened, he was ruined.

Fear and desperation made him do things that looked brave—or at least foolhardy.

With Morn, he spent an inordinately long time in Mallorys, buying drinks that only tightened the knot in his stomach, glowering ferociously at everyone who addressed him, seething under Nick's gaze and ignoring it. But when Nick got up to leave with his crew, his retinue, Angus also heaved upright, snarled Morn to his side.

Without much difficulty, he contrived to arrive in the doorway in time to block Nick's way.

In fact, it seemed a little too easy. Angus' instincts were shrill with alarm. Nick seemed to want this encounter as much as he did.

But he couldn't back down; not now. He was too scared.

"After you, Captain Succorso," he growled, making no effort to disguise his malice. "I know you're in a hurry."

Nick bowed gracefully, but didn't move. "On the contrary, Captain Thermo-pile." Except for his scars, his expression was bland. "I'm in no hurry at all. Please—" he gestured expansively—"after you."

His gaze and his bow and his gesture were all aimed at Morn.

"Ther-*mop*-a-lee," Angus retorted. "Ther-*mop*-a-lee. Get it right, Succorso."

"Really?" Nick cocked a self-assured eyebrow. Apparently he liked the situation. Perhaps it was a kind of stim he especially enjoyed, an adrenaline rush. "Right here in the door? Extraordinary.

"You're plotting, Captain Thermo-pile. You're hatching something. You've got it in your pocket right now. Or are you just playing with yourself?

"Why don't you open up about it? Let someone in to help you."

In one way, Angus seemed to go blind with rage. Playing? *Playing?* But in another, he'd never been clearer, calmer. I'll show you who's *playing*.

He was at his best when he was terrified.

Nick and his retinue—three men, two women—were unarmed; otherwise they wouldn't have been allowed into Mallorys. But they didn't need needle-lasers or old-fashioned shivs against one man. And they were ready to fight for their captain, at any time, in any place. What he'd done to deserve that kind of loyalty, Angus couldn't imagine. But he didn't doubt that the six of them would relish beating him into the deck-plates.

Outside Mallorys, the wide public passages of DelSec were deserted. It was the time of day when most people either drank or stayed in their quarters. Assuming that anybody on Com-Mine Station would have been willing to help Angus in a fight, that help wasn't available now.

He let Nick see him swallow, hesitate. Then he said, "Let's talk about it outside." Deliberately he copied Nick's gesture. "After you."

"No, I insist." Nick grinned. "*I'm* after *you*."

"The hell you are," Angus muttered. "You don't care about me. You're after her." Then he shouldered ahead of Nick through the doorway.

In his pocket, one of his fingers tapped Morn's zone-implant control, sending a spasm through her muscles, a neural storm that looked like violence. As a result, she blocked the exit behind Nick as if she was on Angus' side and wanted to fight for him.

At the same time, Angus pivoted on Nick, grabbed him by his shipsuit, and slung him like a duffel bag around and against the wall.

Surprise and strength gave him all the advantage he needed. With the back of his hand, he struck Nick across the side of his head—a blow that cracked and echoed in the passage like a rivet shearing under stress. The blow made Nick crumple; but Angus held him up and struck him again.

Then he was out of time.

Nick's retinue burst out of Mallorys, knocking Morn to the deck. They were hot for blood.

Angus faced them as if he were calm. With his hands, he dangled Nick's unconscious form in front of them. His fingers were wrapped around their captain's neck.

"Go fucking back inside." His voice sounded like an amiable mine-hammer. "Leave me fucking alone. I'm not fucking done with him."

For a second, Nick's crew faltered, chagrin on their faces.

Then the two women jerked Morn up from the deck and clamped hands to her windpipe.

Morn continued thrashing. Now she looked like she was seriously fighting for her life. Her eyes took in everything; she understood how Angus was using her. But she couldn't stop her struggles.

"Standoff," a man said. "You kill him, we kill her."

The danger wrenched Angus' heart. The need to remain still was so acute it nearly broke him. He wanted to drop Nick and charge at the women, hit and crush everybody who stood in his way, everybody who threatened Morn. But that would be suicide. He couldn't beat all five of them before one of them got him. Or Morn. Somehow, he stood where he was and pretended he didn't care.

"You've got it wrong. You kill her, I kill him. I don't want him dead. I'm just protecting myself. Shits like you like six-to-one odds. I don't."

Abruptly he roared with all the force of his rage, *"Put her fucking down!"*

They obeyed. They wanted to save Nick. And—Angus guessed—they didn't want the responsibility of killing the woman Nick desired. They let go of Morn and backed away.

She dropped convulsively to the deck.

While he was still wrestling with his wish to attack them all,

Angus' nerve-beeper tingled, warning him that *Captain's Fancy* had sent out a call for Nick Succorso.

He didn't hesitate. If what he'd just done didn't provoke some action, nothing would. Carelessly he opened his fists and let Nick fall. With the efficiency of long practice, he keyed the commands on the zone implant control which brought Morn back to her feet, restored her control of her limbs. Then he released her.

The way her gaze sprang involuntarily to Nick's sprawled form hurt him worse than anything Nick could have done in a fight.

But *Captain's Fancy*'s crew ignored her now. They didn't try to stop Angus from leaving. Surely they had their own beepers. And their captain needed them.

Without interference, Angus returned Morn to *Bright Beauty* and sealed the hatches.

This time he was determined to do her serious harm. The blows he'd already struck flamed in his arm, burning for repetition. Violence made him hungry for more. He meant to damage her, *needed* to damage her. She deserved it.

But first he checked the computer monitoring *Captain's Fancy*'s Station communications. He wanted to know why Nick was being summoned.

The explanation was in code. *Captain's Fancy* had received one of those messages from Security and immediately requested Nick Succorso's return to his ship.

Cursing as foully as he knew how, Angus Thermopyle abandoned his purpose against Morn Hyland. Something was about to happen. His instincts were shouting at him, yelling at him to *leave,* go at once, escape before Nick could take revenge. But he ignored that warning. There was no way to leave; he was already committed. He ordered Morn to her g-seat, ordered her to strap herself in. Then he keyed his monitor to display current data from *Captain's Fancy*.

He knew it when Nick got aboard.

After that, for some reason *Captain's Fancy* cleared all channels and stopped talking to Station.

Because his instincts clamored like Klaxons, Angus snapped at Morn, "Warm up. Get ready. I think we're going somewhere."

She obeyed the way he liked: correctly, without question or delay. *Bright Beauty*'s systems came alive. Function lights winked awake on his console. Checklists and verifications flickered across the screens. Scanners started to feed running data into the computers: automatic navigational input from Station; information about the presence and movements of ships in Com-Mine Station's control space.

While Morn worked, Angus concentrated on *Captain's Fancy*.

What was Nick doing?

Getting ready. Of course. Getting ready to leave.

But why?

Because Security had told him something.

What?

Angus sucked his upper lip. What had Security told Nick Succorso?

His boards and screens cleared. *Bright Beauty* was prepared to go. Morn sat still, staring at nothing, her hands resting on her console so they could do whatever he told her quickly.

Indecision paralyzed him. He didn't know how to go against his instincts. They'd saved him too often. If he didn't listen to them, he was lost.

He felt the pain; but until he tasted blood, he didn't realize he'd bitten into his lip.

Muttering obscenities automatically, as if they no longer had any meaning, he disconnected his ship from the dummy line which fed him *Captain's Fancy*'s data-stream.

*Bright Beauty*'s communication systems crackled awake. Like every receiver in and around Com-Mine Station, his gear caught the codes and frequencies of a distress call. Immediately his speakers broadcast the call.

It froze him in his seat. One part of his mind went completely blank with surprise and alarm as the incoming supply ship from Earth cried for help. Navigational computer wrecked. Somebody on the crew crazy with gap-sickness. Coordinates lost. Control lost. Crisis urgent. Triangulate and pursue. Distressdistressdis—

But the rest of him was thinking furiously.

Incoming supply ship. The richest treasure this side of an asteroid full of pure cesium. And it was weeks early. Probably a trick to protect it from pirates.

That was what Security was talking to Nick Succorso about. Telling him the ship would be early. So he would have a clear shot at it. The change of schedule would backfire. The ship wouldn't be expecting his attack.

But nobody could have predicted this emergency. Any second now, Station was going to slap a curfew on the docks, forbidding anyone to leave—making it a life offense for anyone to leave—until an official rescue mission could be organized. If he didn't move fast, Nick would lose his chance—

With his heart triphammering and a rush of sweat soaking his shipsuit, Angus snapped into action.

The distress call went dead only a few seconds later. Apparently the damage to the navigational computer had spread to communications. But by that time he'd already dropped all his lines and uncoupled from Station. By some definitions, he was no longer in dock; he still had to obey Center, but he wasn't legally bound by Security.

His scan told him *Captain's Fancy* was doing the same.

Station took a different view of the situation, of course. Center wanted absolute command over every ship in its control space; Security wanted authority over any rescue or salvage. Angus' receivers picked up a burst of static; the orders blared in his ears.

"*Bright Beauty,* this is Station Center. You must redock. An emergency has been declared. Emergency procedures are in force. You may not depart.

"If you ignore this instruction"—Angus heard satisfaction in the metallic voice—"we will be forced to consider you illegal. You will be fired upon."

Typical authoritarian attitude—arrogant and unjustified. Like the UMC cops and Security, Station Center was in love with muscle. Unfortunately, that didn't change anything. Angus would still die when the Station started shooting.

*Captain's Fancy* must have received the same orders. Nick ignored them. Blithely, as if she were deaf or invulnerable, his ship pivoted into her normal escape attitude for departure; under easy thrust, she ran out a few dozen kilometers from Station—directly into prime range for Com-Mine's cannon.

She waited for the first warning shots to be fired. Then she winked off Angus' screens; disappeared as completely as if she'd ceased to exist.

He watched and swore, helpless to stop her.

At the same time, however, he didn't let anything interfere with his own actions. *Bright Beauty* was already in her escape attitude, and he was pulling her out from the Station with all the thrust she was known to have.

The shit-eaters in Center had that one chance to kill him, but they missed it. As required by law, they sent their first shots across his trajectory, to warn him.

At once, he fed stutter into his drive and started transmitting his own distress call.

*There's a short somewhere. Smoke. Controls locked—I can't navigate. Don't shoot. I'm trying to come around.*

That froze Center. They didn't have any choice: they had to wait to see whether he was telling the truth.

While his call went out, he growled to Morn, "Brace yourself. This is going to hurt."

Steeling himself in his g-seat, he engaged *Bright Beauty*'s power boosters.

After that, Com-Mine's guns couldn't track him. He wasn't literally moving too fast for their capabilities: he was simply moving faster than anyone could believe. Surely his ship wasn't built for that kind of acceleration? By the time Center adjusted its preconceptions—and its targ programming—*Bright Beauty* was out of range.

Angus and Morn were unconscious, of course. The stress was too much to sustain. But the ship's boosters cut off after a preset interval, reducing g to more tolerable levels; and in the meantime, *Bright Beauty*'s automatic helm set her course by tracing the supply ship's distress call back along its transmission vector.

Angus recovered first. He stayed where he was, however, breathing deeply and trying to clear his head. Made it. Once again, his ship had saved him. Hurt as she was, she was *his*. If he had to, he would make the entire Station pay for the damage done to her. No one was allowed to harm anything *his*.

A short time later, Morn twitched, groaned, lifted her head. Unconsciousness and the strain of g took a moment to fade from her eyes. Then, without hesitation, she put her hands on her console and started tapping in instructions.

He was too stunned and relieved; and too much time had passed: he'd forgotten the danger. He wasn't looking at his own console, so he didn't see the blip which began to flash as soon as she set to work.

Luckily, he glanced over at her and saw the look of rapture on her face.

That look was unmistakable.

*The whole inside of my head was different. I was floating, and everything was clear. It was like the universe spoke to me.*

In sudden panic, he slapped at his console, identified the alert.

She was trying to feed a self-destruct sequence into *Bright Beauty*'s engines.

Bitch. Fucking daughter of a fucking whore.

Gap-sickness.

He was too tired to swear at her aloud. The thought of her illness made him weary and slightly nauseous. A strange burning sensation filled his eyes. He should have gone over to her and hit her, of course, should have pounded her back into her right mind. But he was too tired for that. And anyway, *Bright Beauty* was running under spin. Sighing as if he were sad, he activated the zone-implant control.

Morn's hands fell off the console, and she slumped in her g-seat.

That was necessary; he had to do it. When he engaged *Captain's Fancy,* he couldn't take the risk that she might interfere somehow, hamper or weaken him. There was no reason why he shouldn't switch her off like a robot with its power supply cut.

And yet he felt about her gap-sickness the same way he felt about *Bright Beauty*'s wounded side.

Somebody was going to pay for it. He would get even with the entire parsec if he had to.

In the meantime, however, he had to take care of himself. He was confident that the place where the supply ship stopped transmitting was at least half a day away under strong thrust: ships crossing the gap were required to reenter normal space that far from any station, to minimize the chance of an accident. And his scanners would warn him as soon as he crossed the supply ship's particle trail. So he had time for some food and a little rest. If he weren't at his best, he might not be able to beat *Captain's Fancy*.

He was relying on surprise. Nick Succorso couldn't know his data-stream had been tapped. And he couldn't know *Bright Beauty* had been able to get away from Com-Mine Station.

He couldn't know Angus Thermopyle had no interest at all in the supply ship.

Without gap capability, *Bright Beauty* lacked *Captain's Fancy*'s ability to leave Com-Mine and the belt for some other star system or station, someplace where she wasn't known. For that reason, Angus couldn't risk an attack on the supply ship. If he found her, he would be forced to rescue her crew and salvage her cargo in the legally prescribed manner. DelSec lived on those supplies as much as the rest of Station did. If he pirated them—and DelSec was given any reason of any kind to believe he'd done it—he would be murdered the next time he set foot in Mallorys.

No, Angus was after Nick himself. What he wanted was to

catch Nick gutting the lost ship. If he could do that, all his options were good—as long as he destroyed *Captain's Fancy*. He could rescue the crew (if Nick had left any of them alive); keep as much of the cargo as he wanted for himself ("lost in combat"); salvage the rest; go back to Com-Mine like a hero.

His instincts assured him this was the wrong thing to do.

He ignored them.

First he stopped *Bright Beauty*'s spin and went to get himself a quick meal. Then he returned to his g-seat and began testing all his sensors and sifters and sniffers to make sure they were in proper tune.

Whenever he chewed on his upper lip, he tasted blood again.

CHAPTER 14

T hree hours sooner than Angus was expecting, the alarm linked to his tracking gear chimed.

He grunted in surprise. It was too soon. The supply ship should never have crossed back into normal space this close to the Station.

And that wasn't all. Ignoring g, he hauled *Bright Beauty* around and dropped spin to improve his scan. The particle trace didn't look right. Big haulers like supply ships had throatier engines: they left a wider track across the dark, more garbage at the fringes and more complete dispersion in the core. Studying his displays and readouts made him so suspicious that he felt like throwing up.

And yet—

The sheer coincidence of another ship having passed directly across the supply ship's transmission vector was staggering.

And if this *was* the supply ship's trace, he was much closer to her than he'd anticipated. She was closer to Com-Mine; therefore her distress call had taken less time to reach Station; therefore she'd had less time to blunder away from this spot; therefore he could catch up with her more easily.

And by rights Nick's departure from Station should have taken him well past this point. It was virtually impossible to cut a blink crossing this short. Which meant he was already out where the ship should be. If the ship was there, Angus might not be able to catch him in time. But if the ship was *here*—

If the ship was here, Angus could get to her first. Nick would have to come back looking for her.

The perfect situation for an ambush.

Angus' dilemma was terrifying. If he guessed wrong, he would lose his only chance to take *Captain's Fancy* by surprise. Then he would have to live with the consequences of his earlier attack on Nick. And Nick had Security on his side. He had a newer ship. He had an entire crew to back him up. Angus might be forced to hide out in the belt for years.

His sweat made him stink like a swine. Nevertheless he knew exactly what to do. Focusing scan back along the trace, he went looking for the characteristic burst of radiation and dimensional emission which accompanied every crossing from the gap into normal space.

Before long, he found it.

There: the supply ship had entered normal space right there. She was too much of everything—too soon, too close, too easily crippled; her trace was too narrow. But she was *there,* where he could get to her hours ahead of his enemy.

Giving *Bright Beauty* as much boost as he could stomach, he reversed course and followed the trace.

When he plotted the ship's speed from the density of the particle trail, he saw she was decelerating slowly. That made sense. Unable to navigate, she would naturally want to reduce her own momentum so she would be easier to catch and board. Instead of pushing ahead, however, he began to cut his own speed correspondingly. He didn't want the supply ship to know he'd found her. She might try to beacon him—and that might betray his position. He intended to sneak up on her, hovering just outside normal scan range and playing dead so he wouldn't show up on *Captain's Fancy*'s instruments. He even went so far as to ride straight down the center of the supply ship's trace, confusing it with *Bright Beauty*'s to hide himself.

He would wait until Nick came. He would wait until *Captain's Fancy* cut the supply ship's heart out, eliminated embarrassing witnesses, arranged easy access to the cargo. He would wait until Nick docked with the supply ship's carcass.

Then he would rip Nick Succorso and everything that bastard loved down to raw electrons and space dust.

He intended to release Morn Hyland so she could watch. He would let her see the blast and try to guess which piece of incinerated debris represented the man she wanted instead of him.

After that—if she was lucky—he would strip off her shipsuit and make her do things that sickened her. He would teach her who owned her until she was in no danger of ever forgetting it.

If she wasn't lucky, he might do a little surgery on her, rearrange parts of her body somewhat, just for fun.

First, however, he had to find the supply ship.

He didn't understand it: she kept slowing and slowing—and yet she remained out of scan-range, invisible somewhere ahead of him. At her present rate of deceleration, he should be almost on top of her by now. Yet he couldn't locate her.

That was impossible. He knew for a fact that his equipment was capable of tracking down one lost EVA suit in a hundred thousand cubic kilometers of black emptiness. The supply ship couldn't hide from him, even if she had a reason to try, which of course she didn't because she was dead unless somebody came to her rescue, she had to be here *somewhere,* had to be—

When he found the explanation, it stunned him for a few seconds.

That much delay nearly killed him.

Ahead of *Bright Beauty,* a sudden powerful roar along the trace showed that the ship he was following had cut in full thrust, enough sheer power to pull away from him at an acceleration of several g.

Which was why he hadn't caught up with her. She'd been piling up speed while he'd been slowing down.

But that was crazy. No crippled supply ship would do something like that. A crippled supply ship with runaway thrusters would jettison her engines rather than let herself race out of reach of help.

Therefore the ship he followed wasn't a crippled supply ship.

He'd been tricked. There was no supply ship. The distress call was a ruse. He'd set out intending to spring an ambush; but the ambush had been sprung on him, he was already caught—

Stunned, he stared at his readouts and displays, and for a moment he didn't move. The extent to which he'd been duped paralyzed him. What chance did he have against people who could do *this*? He'd been so thoroughly outmaneuvered that he was as good as dead.

Gaping dismay, he looked over at Morn.

She hadn't moved, of course. The zone implant blocked the neural impulses which connected her mind to her body. She was conscious, but helpless. Like his ship. Unless he could find a way to save them, they would both be destroyed.

A howl rose in his throat; but he had no time for it.

*Bright Beauty* had been running without spin. And all his attention had been focused on the particle trace. He hauled her into a turn, bringing sensors and sniffers to bear on her blind spot.

At once, her Klaxons went off, wailing like the damned.

A ship came at him fast. No, worse than that: the ship had already fired, throwing a flight of torpedoes in his direction at terrible speed.

His terror was absolute: it made him superhuman. *Bright Beauty* was still turning, still starting into spin. He gathered boost and unleashed it at an angle, kicked her to the side so hard that she tumbled away as if she were totally out of control, wheeling like a derelict.

Every alarm she had on her seemed to go off simultaneously. She wasn't made for stress like that. Damaged as she was, she was in danger of breaking apart.

But the torpedoes missed.

Under so much g, he should have gone completely blank; crushed unconscious in his seat. It should have been impossible for him to retain any sense of orientation, of the spatial relationship between himself and his attacker.

Nevertheless, while *Bright Beauty* tumbled, he opened fire.

The spray of his matter cannon went miraculously close to the other ship. She was forced to veer off.

He had no way of identifying his attacker, but she was almost certainly the ship he'd been following—almost certainly *Captain's Fancy*. Somehow, Nick Succorso had been able to cut his blink crossing short enough to intersect the transmission vector of the bogus distress call. Or he'd blinked far enough past that point to return with another crossing. He'd lured Angus to follow him. Then, when he'd slowed Angus nearly to a standstill, he'd accelerated and looped back to attack.

None of that mattered, of course. It didn't matter who Angus' enemy was—not now. The only thing that mattered was that he was trapped and had to fight for his life.

For his life and *Bright Beauty*'s. And Morn's.

His ship's tumble was dangerous. It was also much too slow. Under this kind of g, he couldn't read his screens. Still he knew somehow what the other ship was doing, where she was in relation to him.

As his attacker came around and brought her guns to bear, he hit braking thrust, straightened out *Bright Beauty*'s fall, got her tubes behind her, and gave her as much drive as he thought he could stand without losing his mind to the dark.

Matter fire licked her sides, but didn't do any real damage. Then she pulled out of range, surprising her attacker with the fact that she was still under control and could perform maneuvers which should have been impossible.

Angus' head was jammed brutally against his g-seat; but now at least he could look at his displays and screens, his console. Targ plotted the other ship automatically, showing her on a grid even a crazy could have understood.

She was gaining on him. At this rate, she would be in position to open fire in a matter of seconds.

Angus ought to be taking evasive action.

But he already knew *Captain's Fancy* was fast. If he really wanted to outrun her, he would have to give *Bright Beauty* all the power his drive could generate. Then he would black out. He wouldn't know whether he was alive or dead until his ship reached the end of her fuel and stopped accelerating.

He didn't pile on any more boost.

He also didn't take any evasive action. To do that, he would have to slow down; or else the inertial stress might be enough to make him hemorrhage.

Instead he started seeding the space behind him with static-mines.

He didn't know it, but his mouth and chin were covered with blood. Every time he bit his upper lip, it bled more.

Static-mines were tiny: a scan officer with his mind on other things might miss them. Angus released them in clusters of ten or twelve, but they scattered so quickly that they shouldn't create a combined blip for the attacking ship to read.

If she fired at him and hit one—

Or if she simply ran into it—

She fired. His displays showed him the characteristic energy-burst of matter cannon. *Bright Beauty* was struck—another scar along her flank. Yet she was lucky: the hurt was no worse than a slap.

The salvo also caught a few of the static-mines.

He'd keyed them to set each other off. In seconds, his trail was covered by disruptive explosions, a barrage of particle noise, doppler signals, and radio garbage loud enough to randomize every scanner *Captain's Fancy* had.

In effect, *Bright Beauty*—and space itself—disappeared. The attacking ship was left deaf and blind.

She would stay that way for ten or fifteen seconds, until her computers were able to filter the chaos, distinguish between noise and fact.

At that instant, Angus wrenched *Bright Beauty* to the side, away from her former course. He gave her one quick slam of extra boost.

Then he shut her down.

Everything. Even life-support. Thrust; communication; lights; sensors: everything except minimal computer function and passive scan systems which didn't give out signs of life; everything except the faint, almost undetectable nuclear hum of charged matter cannon.

He was trying to make himself invisible.

Trying to compensate for the fact that he was outgunned and outmanned and probably outpowered.

Sweat drenched his shipsuit, but he didn't notice that. He forgot to curse; he almost refused to breathe because in his imagination he could taste his air already starting to go bad. His whole body was focused on the dull screens of his passive scan—sifters which sent out nothing, but only accepted and interpreted what came to them across the void. Where was his attacker? By rights, his sense of space told him, she should be *there*. But his equipment said nothing. He was as blind as *Captain's Fancy*. The only difference, the only hope, was that *Captain's Fancy* was the one in pursuit, that—

The only difference was that she was still moving under power.

His screens flickered. *There*.

Moving cautiously now, hunting, groping—but still using her engines, life-support, internal communications; still sending a shout of data through the residual noise left by the static-mines.

Because she didn't know where he was, she was about to come under his guns.

*Come on, you bastards.*

He didn't so much as whisper aloud: he was irrationally afraid his attacker might hear him.

*Come on, you sons of whores. Let me have just one good shot at you. Just one.*

His ship made no sound, gave away nothing except the small hum of her guns. Surely the only way Nick could spot her was by picking out her silhouette against the starfield? And surely they were far enough away from each other to make that difficult, nearly impossible? Surely it would take time for the computers to run that kind of analysis on what they saw?

Time: all Angus needed was time. His attacker was already within range. If he fired now, he wouldn't miss. But he might not kill her. If he waited until she came closer, he would have a chance to catch her with a torpedo.

Just one torpedo would be enough to break her back. He was sure of that. He knew what his torpedos could do.

He waited.

*Come on, you shithead motherfucking cocksuckers.*

Waited.

Too late, his equipment registered the sudden blast of power as the other ship fed boost to her thrusters.

She'd spotted him. Just when he was about to gut her, tear her entirely to pieces, she'd spotted him. Or she'd guessed what he was doing.

With all her strength, she accelerated out of his way.

Raging, he jabbed at his guns, sent cannon fire like hate at her, hot and savage, frantic for destruction. One entire barrage got her, skimming open the metal skin of her side, spilling atmosphere and debris into the vacuum. But that wasn't enough to kill her.

He knew it wasn't enough because she kept returning his fire until she pulled out of range.

And she hit him.

He didn't have time to assess the damage: he had to get moving, had to get *Bright Beauty* under thrust before his attacker could turn. Fiercely, he brought her back to life, ignited her engines.

He knew his ship. She was *his,* and he'd taken care of her intimately for years. When his thrusters roared alive, he knew instantly that one of them had been hurt. It stuttered and choked, sending a terrible shudder through the hull.

That last hit had holed one of his thruster tubes.

The side-blast would make *Bright Beauty* almost impossible to control.

He tried: brutally, desperately, he tried. Ignoring the strain on his body, his heart, the strain on Morn, the strain on every suture of *Bright Beauty*'s skin and every weld of her frame, he fought for speed and control, wrestled with the side-blast for his life.

It was no good. He couldn't do it. It would have taken all his skill just to run her in a straight line at a limp. While his attacker turned and scanned him and studied the situation and then started back toward him to finish him off, he accomplished nothing except a wild cartwheel into the dark, an off-center spin that made *Bright Beauty* completely unmanageable. Now if he tried for speed the only thing he would do was rip his own mind away so that he would be unconscious when he died.

He didn't know what to do. He didn't know how to fail and die, but that was his only alternative. While *Bright Beauty* reeled out of control like this, he couldn't so much as fire his guns. They were useless. And he knew his enemy was closing on him, knew it without a glance at scan—which was hopelessly confused in any case. By the time he succeeded at pulling his ship out of her spin, Nick Succorso would be ready to blast him to dust.

Only because *Bright Beauty*'s motion was so painful, he struggled with it. He shut down the engine with the damaged tube, then used braking against the spin. But when her screens cleared, he saw that he'd done nothing except make life easier for his enemy.

The other ship was in position: poised; primed.

For the second time, he found himself staring down the pitiless gullet of enemy cannon.

The sight made him want to weep.

There was nothing he could do. All his anger and inspiration were gone, expended. His attacker was within range now, but it wasn't worth the trouble to fire at her. He might be able to scar her a little, that was all. A few scars wouldn't prevent her from eviscerating him and his ship and everything he'd ever wanted.

Abruptly, a communication channel crackled.

"Captain Thermo-pile."

Nick Succorso. Of course.

"You're beaten. Remember that. I warned you."

Angus had the distinct impression Nick was laughing at him.

Without another shot, *Captain's Fancy* shifted course and started to pull away.

He couldn't believe it. He stared at his displays, his readouts. His cameras couldn't see far enough to be sure; but all his sensors agreed with each other. *Captain's Fancy* had turned her back on him. With taunting ease, she ran out of his reach almost immediately. He was left alone and damaged.

He felt like he'd been marooned. For the second time, he had no idea why he was alive.

# CHAPTER 15

**B**right Beauty's life-support didn't seem to be working well enough. His mouth was full of sand. The whole inside of his head was a desert. *You're beaten.* He wasn't angry anymore. *Remember that.* He didn't have any hope. *I warned you.* Something had been taken away from him—something he needed and couldn't define and didn't know how to live without.

His ship was crippled. He'd been gone from Com-Mine Station for less than twelve hours, but he would be lucky to get back in thirty-six.

Morn Hyland still slumped in her g-seat, deaf and blind to everything.

He couldn't afford to have *Bright Beauty* fixed. If he reached Com-Mine in one piece, that would be as far as he went. He couldn't make any money without using her, and she was in no condition to be used. He was trapped; there was no escape. He might as well have been marooned—

It was Morn's fault, of course. None of this would have happened to him—or to his ship—if she hadn't conceived a passion for Nick Succorso.

And yet he wasn't angry.

He wanted to be angry. If he could get angry, maybe he would be able to think of something.

After staring at his screens for a long time, he keyed the parallel control to Morn's zone implant and let her have her body back.

Trying to be angry, he didn't look at her. Instead, he let his hurt, numb thoughts wander to the question of how much she remembered, how much she knew about what had happened. She'd been in the grip of her gap-sick vision, the message from the universe commanding self-destruction, when he activated her zone implant. Had she been lost in mad clarity all this time? Was she still sick? Or had she been capable of seeing, absorbing, understanding?

She twisted against her seat, stretched her muscles, studied her console and the displays. Involuntarily he turned to watch her. Her features were pale and concentrated. Then, by degrees, horror crept into her face—the horror he recognized.

In a stark and absolute whisper, she asked, "Did I do that?"

He should have let her believe she was responsible. That would be worse than anything physical he could do to her. She was horrified of him, of course, revolted to the core and helpless; but to fear herself like that, to be revolted again at herself like that, to be helpless against her own destructiveness—that would be worse. It would be as bad as what he'd been striving for until the moment when she and Nick first saw each other—as bad as finding in herself the knowledge that she needed what he did to her and loved it.

She deserved to believe she was responsible.

He couldn't do it; he had no idea why. Part of his brain was still planning what he would say to pin the blame on her as he replied, "Succorso got us. A trap—there was no supply ship. You can see the damage." Her console would give her all the details she needed.

For several moments she didn't say anything. Her relief was so strong that she seemed unable to think. But then, slowly, she began to frown.

Keeping her voice neutral, she asked, "Why are we still alive?"

Angus shrugged as if he were the one who was helpless. "He let us go."

She had to consider that for a while: even in her condition, she could see it didn't make sense. Nick attacked because he wanted to kill Angus. Then why did he leave *Bright Beauty* alive? He set his trap so that he could rescue Morn. Then why didn't he? Why did he risk killing her?

Nevertheless something made sense to her; Angus could read her expression well enough to know it when she reached a conclusion.

Carefully she cleared her throat and said, "You're beaten."

Oh, yes.

"He beat you."

Yes.

"You'll be lucky if you can make this thing crawl back to Station."

The words were fierce, almost vindictive; she might have been gloating. But she didn't sound that way. Her tone was too flat, too well-controlled. If anything, she sounded a little sad, as if she, too, had been hurt in some way.

*Trying* to be angry, he growled, "Proud of him, aren't you. You think that fucker's some kind of hero. *Beat* me. You're counting the minutes until you two"—he had no words strong enough "—until you can screw him."

Abruptly, she licked her lips; she appeared to have trouble swallowing. "Angus." She'd never used his name before. "Angus, listen to me.

"I can save you."

He thought his heart was going to stop beating.

"I'll testify for you. When you go back to Com-Mine, they'll charge you with illegal departure. I'll support you. I'm not much of a cop anymore, but I've still got my id tag. I'll tell them you left on my orders. And I'll tell them there was no supply ship. It was a hoax—that other ship set it up. I'll tell them to arrest Nick Succorso. I can't save your ship, but I can save you."

Tell them? Turn on Nick Succorso? Give up that piece of meat for me? Impossible. Angus felt sure he was losing his mind. For me?

"Just give me the control." Her voice was husky, full of need. "The zone-implant control."

Then he understood. Shit, how he wished he could be angry! She wanted the control. It wasn't for him. Nothing was for him. She wanted all that power for herself. Power *over* herself—power to be whatever she wanted. No gap-sickness. No fear: immune to fear. And no consequences for all the harm he'd done her. The perfect cop. The perfect lover. As close as human flesh could come to immortality.

He'd broken her in ways he hadn't anticipated. Her damage was as profound as *Bright Beauty*'s.

He had trouble seeing. His eyes ran and wouldn't stop. "You're crazy," he rasped as if he were weeping. "That's as illegal as what I did to you. You're a cop. Your whole family will be discredited, heroic Captain Davies Hyland and his reputation shot to hell."

She reacted bitterly. "What does that matter?" she retorted. "They're *dead*."

Angus tried a different tack.

"You aren't thinking straight. You're a *cop*. It's worse when a cop breaks the law. They'll crucify you. Mandatory death penalty. They'll find out. They have to find out. And then you'll be finished."

Behind his tears, he could see her in lockup; see her waiting to be executed, vaporized. As precious as *Bright Beauty*.

"I'll lose my ship."

"You can't save it," she shot back, suddenly angry, more than a little desperate. "I can handle Station Security. And the UMCP. I'll think of a way. But *nothing* can save your ship. It's too badly broken. We'll need a miracle just to get back to Com-Mine alive."

"Please. Give me the control." Now she was pleading nakedly. "I'm not going to use it against you. I need it to heal."

He tried to clear his vision. Softly he said, "And give up my ship. That's the deal, isn't it. You'll save me. If I let you have the control. But I have to give up my ship."

My life.

She nodded. After a moment, she replied, "What else have you got to bargain with?"

At last, something like his old energy came back to him. Roughly he undid the straps and pushed his bulk out of his g-seat. He needed to be angry at her one last time, needed to hate her the way he'd always hated her, the way he hated everyone.

He went toward her.

Clamping one hand on the armrest of her seat, bracing his feet on the deck, he struck her a blow like the one which had felled Nick, a blow with the whole weight of his existence behind it. If her seat hadn't absorbed some of the impact, she might have been knocked unconscious. He might have broken her neck.

"Bitch. I'll never give up my ship."

Red welled in her cheek; blood trickled from the cuts of her teeth inside her mouth. Pain and shock glazed her eyes: for a moment, she couldn't focus them.

But she made no effort to defend herself. If he wanted to hit her again, she was there.

He couldn't do it. It was like hurting *Bright Beauty*. She was too beautiful. The stark red line of blood across her fine skin wrung his heart. He needed rage and violence, but they were gone.

"Now *you* listen to *me*," he panted as if he were groaning. "It's impossible. You couldn't get away with it.

"Maybe you can get them to believe you ordered me to violate Center's orders so you could come out here after Succorso. But they won't believe anything else unless you file charges. If you don't, your credibility's gone. Then you're in the same shit I am. Only you'll be suspect for destroying *Starmaster*. If they find evidence of self-destruct, you'll be court-martialed. They'll find the zone implant *and* the control, and then you're dead.

"You'll have to file charges.

"But if you do that, you'll have to give them my datacore. Otherwise you don't have any evidence." He could survive that— he could retain his life, if not his freedom—but she didn't know that. And he had a horror of lockup. Imprisonment alone might be enough to ruin him. "You'll end up killing me.

"And if you do all that, they'll still find the implant and the control.

"*Think* about it. After what you've been through, they're going to give you a physical. They're going to insist on it. If you resist, they'll get suspicious—they'll force it on you. No matter what you do, you're dead.

"You're going to have to play this out the way it is.

"I'm trying to save your life too."

Now he wasn't able to meet her dull, smoldering gaze. Slowly he pushed back to his seat. He strapped himself in. His movements were abrupt, jerky, as if he didn't have them entirely under control; as if he could have used a zone implant himself.

"We've got a holed thruster tube," he muttered. "It'll take everything I can do just to make her run in a straight line. You'll have to handle everything else."

Glowering like one of the lost, he routed most of his command functions to her console. Then he concentrated all the determination he had left on making *Bright Beauty* go where he wanted.

He knew Morn would do her part. What choice did she have?

But he also knew what he'd done to her. He'd destroyed her last hope. And he'd hit her again, after all his gentleness; after his gentleness had almost persuaded her he could be reached.

He understood the consequences.

Now she had no choice but to help destroy him.

CHAPTER 16

Two days and more after her departure, *Bright Beauty* sputtered back into dock at Com-Mine Station.

The trip was harder and longer than Angus had anticipated. For the first time since Morn started crewing for him, he needed drugs to stay alert.

In fact, she accepted stim herself. The chore of maintaining the ship while he navigated wasn't exhausting, but his refusal to stop for rest wore her down. She had a hot glitter in her eyes and a feverish patch of color on each cheek as he settled *Bright Beauty* into the berth Center assigned; she looked like a woman whose life was on the line.

He noticed that. Despite his own fatigue and the muzzy-headedness of drugs, he noticed everything about her. She needed sleep.

If he could have let her have it, he would have.

Unfortunately, there were Station inspectors pounding at his hatches. He'd ignored an order of curfew to go off after *Captain's Fancy*. And the supply ship was still missing. The official search hadn't found anything. And *Captain's Fancy* hadn't returned. A board of inquiry wanted to ask Angus Thermopyle questions. Until he answered them, he was effectively under arrest.

He couldn't afford sleep. And he couldn't afford to let Morn sleep. He needed her to back him up again.

He keyed off his console and got out of his g-seat, swearing uselessly at the force of Station gravity. "Shut her down," he told Morn. "We're going to be here for a while." Then he added, "Don't say anything. I'll handle the fucking inspectors. You just sit there and do your best to look like a cop."

She nodded once, tightly. With her hands on the console, she got to work rigging *Bright Beauty* for rest.

Angus was afraid he would never be able to warm his ship up again. But even that fear was good for something. Relying on it because he had so little anger or strength, he went to let the inspectors aboard.

They had a lot to say to him: they made a number of demands.

For once, what he told them came close to the exact truth.

I don't give a shit about the supply ship. I was after Nick Succorso.

Really? A treasure like that—just waiting to be looted? Do you expect us to believe that, Captain Thermopyle?

Do you think I'm crazy? A supply ship? Angus didn't have to fake his exasperation. If I put one finger on her, the sewage in DelSec would have me for breakfast. And I sure as hell wouldn't come back here. With a treasure like that, I could buy all the repairs I need somewhere else.

Then what were you doing?

I already told you. I was after Succorso.

Why?

Deliberately Angus looked at Morn. That also was the truth, but it had the effect of a lie. Snarling, he said, *Succorso* was after the supply ship.

How do you know?

Shit! Why the fucking hell do you think he broke curfew and blinked out of here? Why do you think he hasn't come back?

All right. What happened?

I never found the supply ship. He attacked me. Holed my thruster tube. The only thing I've done since then is crawl back here.

Why did he attack you?

With difficulty, Angus refrained from yelling. Take a guess.

Are you sure it was him?

No. You got any ideas who else would jump me out in the middle of fucking nowhere for no fucking reason?

The inspectors shrugged as if the list of people who might fit that description were endless.

You broke curfew, Captain Thermopyle. That charge will stick. You weren't docked, but you were in Station control space. You'll have to surrender your datacore.

The hell I will. I told you. I was after Succorso.

That changes nothing. You broke curfew.

I had orders. Again Angus turned his glare on Morn. I couldn't obey them and you too.

Still she didn't say anything. This time, however, she took out her UMCP id tag for the inspectors to worry about.

Faced with the unexplained possibilities she represented—the possibility, for instance, that she'd commandeered Angus Thermopyle's ship to pursue Nick Succorso despite the curfew—the inspectors couldn't shake Angus' story. They searched *Bright Beauty* as well as they could without knowing her secrets, but they didn't find anything. Finally they looked at the damaged thruster tube. It seemed to give them a certain amount of satisfaction.

If Captain Succorso comes in, we'll treat him the same way we did you. If we find anything from that ship—anything at all—we'll lock him up for the rest of his natural life. But if he's clean, we're not going to charge him for shooting at you. Not unless you can prove it was him. The inspectors smiled humorlessly. Not unless you hand over your datacore and let us read it.

Thanks so much, Angus rasped. You're all heart. It's a pleasure getting justice and decent treatment from you.

But he was too worn-out to feel much relief—or any hope. The ability to bluff the inspectors didn't solve his problems.

He was forbidden to leave Station, of course, but that was a minor inconvenience under the circumstances. When the board of inquiry granted him temporary permission to disembark and make use of Com-Mine Station's facilities, he escorted the inspectors off *Bright Beauty* and sealed the hatches. Then he put Morn to bed asleep and climbed into his bunk because there was nothing else he could do.

A few hours later, he woke up in a sweat of alarm; a knife against his heart told him he'd forgotten something, neglected something. Something deadly. He seemed to be waking up from a dream in which a terrible mistake was made clear to him.

Now, however, what that mistake was drifted out of his grasp while his lungs heaved and his chest pounded. *Bright Beauty's* air conditioning chilled the sweat on his skin, but didn't do anything to cool off his fright.

Maybe it was just Station gravity weighing him down, making

him feel leaden and defeated; maybe he was getting too old to shift easily between the presence and absence of g. He wasn't used to thinking of himself as either old or young. In fact, he didn't often pay much attention to his physical organism. But now he tried to comfort himself with physiological speculations.

He was getting old. He was having trouble adjusting to Station g. That was all.

No.

He'd forgotten something.

Nick's taunts came back to him.

*You're beaten. Remember that. I warned you.*

He still had no idea why Nick let him live.

Neglected something.

He went back to the beginning to try to reason it out.

The explanation had to do with Morn, of course. Nothing else made sense. Nick let him live because killing him would kill her as well. Nick was willing to risk her during the fight, for the sake of beating Angus Thermopyle, for the sake of repaying what Angus did to him; but after he won, he held back so she wouldn't be hurt.

Really? Did that make sense?

Maybe not; but it was good enough to ease Angus' distress a little. Rolling heavily out of his bunk, he scratched at the itch of sweat and grime inside his shipsuit, used the head, dabbed antiseptic from the sickbay on his swollen lip, and lumbered into the command module.

Almost at once, he saw the blip signaling automatically on his board.

He froze.

It was one of the alerts he'd programmed to warn him if Morn tried anything off-limits at her console.

For a moment—just for a moment—he didn't care what the

alert actually was. He was stunned by the impossibility of the situation. He'd never given her a chance to do anything. He watched her all the time. When *Bright Beauty* was shut down, there wasn't any blip. Was that right? He scoured his memory. Yes, that was right. No blip then. And after that he'd put her to sleep. *When* could she have set it off?

No. The recognition hit him harder than the alert itself. He was remembering wrong. He *had* given her a chance.

He'd left her alone in the command module while he went to let the inspectors aboard. And again when they went away. And after that he hadn't so much as glanced at his own controls. He'd been too busy with the inquiry—too tired—

Too beaten—

Oh, shit.

Jerking into motion, he stabbed buttons on his console to identify the alert.

It was so far from what he expected that at first he couldn't believe it. The computer must be making a mistake. Surely she'd done something worse than *that*? Wasn't she trying to kill him, get even with him? Didn't she want to sabotage *Bright Beauty*?

But of course the computer wasn't making a mistake. It showed clearly that Morn had jimmied the locks on one of *Bright Beauty*'s exterior hatches, fixed them so they didn't seal. Then she'd disconnected the automatic signal which warned of an unlocked hatch.

That was ridiculous. His brain reeled, groping. Unselfconsciously he wiped blood off his chin. What had Morn accomplished? The hatch still closed securely. His ship still had integrity against the void.

But now—

—now the hatch could be opened from outside.

Anybody with an EVA suit could sneak aboard.

Anybody with an EVA suit could have sneaked aboard while Angus was asleep.

Shitshitshitshit.

He was so surprised and lost that he jumped to all the wrong conclusions. He checked on Morn first, half-expecting to discover she was already gone. But she still slept where he'd left her under the influence of her zone implant. So then he tuned *Bright Beauty*'s life-sign scanners to read the whole ship for stowaways, hidden murderers, saboteurs.

There was no one else aboard: just Morn and himself.

*You're beaten. Remember that. I warned you.*

Finally panic brought him a burst of inspiration. He went to look in his secret holds.

They were full from deck to ceiling with food, equipment, and medicine.

Every crate and carton bore the seal which identified it as the property of Com-Mine Station—the kind of supplies Com-Mine received from Earth. The kind of supplies a supply ship would carry.

When he went back to the command module and scanned around him, he saw *Captain's Fancy* in dock hardly fifty meters away. She'd come in while he was asleep.

He was trapped. Finished. Dead.

The perfection of it astonished him. No wonder Nick had seemed more than willing to encounter him in the doorway of Mallorys. That gave Nick the chance to say the word "hatch" in front of Morn. And with that slender link between them they found a way to destroy the man they hated.

"Slender" was too strong a word for it. It was slim to the point of nonexistence. Nevertheless Angus believed it instantly.

*You're hatching something.*

What else had she ever had to hope for?

*Why don't you open up about it?*

What else did she have left?

*Let someone in to help you.*

From the moment when she'd heard those words, she must have clung to them, searching them for meaning, chewed them inside and out. In her place, he would have done the same thing. Desperate for rescue, she must have worked like a maniac to find some interpretation which could save her.

And Nick's attack showed her he was serious, showed her she had reason to hope.

That was all she needed. When she got the chance, she did something about it.

No, it wasn't enough. It might have been enough for Morn in her desperation, but it wasn't enough for Nick. He would need to *know* she understood him.

What else had he said?

*You've got it in your pocket right now. Or are you playing with yourself?*

Angus had assumed that was a reference to the zone-implant control; a lucky guess. But now another possibility occurred to him. Like everything else Nick had said, it was aimed at Morn.

There had been plenty of time during the scuffle for Nick's people to put a note in Morn's pocket. A note she would have found later, read, and then destroyed.

A note which told her what Nick wanted her to do.

That was why Nick had allowed Angus to arrange their encounter so easily. So that his people could give Morn his message.

The rest of the plot was simple.

There never was a supply ship. No, of course not. The distress call was a fake, engineered by Nick Succorso and his ally in Security. If the supply ship had been genuine, Security could have given him advance warning; but the emergency on which the plot depended couldn't have been predicted. Therefore the whole thing hadn't happened. The distress call had been faked to lure Angus away from Com-Mine—to set the stage for his ruin.

With a way to sneak aboard *Bright Beauty,* did Nick have Angus killed? Did he simply kidnap Morn? Of course not. A murder would have caused serious trouble for Nick. Despite Angus Thermopyle's reputation, Security would have done everything possible to nail his killer—if for no other reason than to demonstrate its own integrity. And if Morn disappeared from *Bright Beauty* while Angus was left alive, Nick would never be able to rest for fear of Angus' revenge.

No, the trap was perfect. By filling *Bright Beauty*'s holds with supplies provided—no doubt—by his ally in Security, Nick was able to arrange for Angus' destruction without risking Morn. Or himself.

Now all he had to do was give the inspectors some evidence that a crime had been committed. Then they would have the legal right to appropriate *Bright Beauty*'s datacore. That would enable them to find the secret holds. It would inform them of the murder of those miners. And it might give them a clue about Morn's zone implant: the sickbay log was blank; but the datacore contained evidence of the parallel control he'd programmed into his board.

A life sentence for the theft of Station supplies. And the death penalty for murder, if not for the use of a zone implant.

And Morn would go free, of course. Straight to Nick Succorso.

The trap was perfect and horrible. Stark panic rushed through Angus: every instinct he had gibbered for action. Without pausing to think—without really realizing what he did—he strapped himself into his g-seat and began to warm up *Bright Beauty*'s engines.

Get away: escape: run. He was a coward; his instincts were compulsory. Undock and get out of here before Security had time to make a formal arrest. They were going to kill him, *kill* him. Get away *now*.

But he'd been forbidden to leave. If he tried to pull away without permission, Com-Mine would fire on him. With a holed thruster tube, he would never be able to evade the station's guns.

*Bright Beauty* would be destroyed.

Morn would be killed.

*Get away!* You fool, you shithead, *go,* GO!

Morn would be killed.

Dismay twisted a cry out of him. He was willing to risk *Bright Beauty*. He'd done it before, when he had to. But Morn—

The last time he hit her, blood welled in her cheek; blood trickled from the cuts of her teeth inside her mouth. Her beauty was marked red. Thinking about her made his guts heave with terror and desire. She was his, his, his, and if he tried to save himself, she would die.

So what? he demanded of his lonely, forsaken life. She's a bitch, and she did this to me so she can go whore with Nick Succorso. Butcher her now, while she's asleep. She deserves it.

That was what he wanted. Every instinct in him wailed for it. Kill her and *go!* Better to get blasted fighting for your life than sit here and let them give you the death penalty while Nick mother-fucking Succorso watches and laughs!

Unfortunately, his body refused to do it.

Shaking wildly, scarcely controllable, his hands discontinued the warm-up, shut *Bright Beauty* down again. For a long time he sat where he was with his palms clamped over his eyes while instinct and terror fired back and forth inside his head like meteors across the dark.

Then, still shaking, he reached out and erased the parallel zone-implant control from his command computer.

He verified that his sickbay log contained nothing incriminating.

He made a few slight adjustments to his datacore, elisions which were theoretically impossible as well as actively illegal, but which he was able to accomplish because his techniques were so subtle.

After that, he woke up Morn Hyland.

She didn't meet his eyes. That wasn't unusual, not in itself; but this time he knew what it meant, oh, he knew what it meant. Briefly she struggled to shake off the effects of sleep.

However, she didn't get out of bed.

With an effort, her mouth produced a crooked smile. If she noticed his stretched and haggard expression, she gave no sign. Instead, she extended her arms toward him as if she'd been dreaming about him.

As if she wanted, actually wanted, to make love to him, despite his power over her; despite the things he'd done to her.

Involuntarily he recoiled. Behind her smile, her face was studiously empty; blank and beautiful; determined to give nothing away. She couldn't know what was going on, of course; not for sure: she could only guess. She had little to pin her hopes on except one short note and the few sentences he and Nick had exchanged in the doorway of Mallorys. And yet she fought for those hopes.

She was trying to distract him, in case he hadn't yet realized what she'd done.

When he saw that, something inside him broke.

For a moment, he hated her. Somewhere, she'd found the one thing he'd always lacked, the courage to meet her doom head-on, to do what she could to control it. And it was Nick she wanted, Nick she did it for; not Angus. Now, however, it made no difference whether he hated her or not; whether he feared her or loved her. He was no longer in command of his own actions. What he said

and did came to him like impulses from outside, abject and unpre-
meditated.

If he tried to get away, he would be killed.

If he didn't try to get away, he would be killed.

"Get up," he rasped without anger or conviction. "We're going
to Mallorys."

Somehow she managed to keep her features expressionless; she
accepted his rejection and rose from the bed without so much as a
flicker of surprise or fright. Watching her, he felt unexpectedly out-
classed, as if the things he had done to her had made her greater
than he was.

It might be too late. Station Security might already be on the
way to arrest him. The control to her zone implant felt like a grenade
in his pocket, primed to destroy him. Nevertheless he went ahead
without hurrying.

After she'd used the head, they left *Bright Beauty* for the last
time and went to DelSec.

CHAPTER 17

Mallorys was crowded. The time was Station evening; rats and cynics of every description had come out of the bulkheads to cadge drinks or sell secrets, share loneliness or court oblivion. Nevertheless Angus Thermopyle didn't have any trouble finding a table. His reputation was bad enough already: nobody wanted to be near him, not while he was suspected of looting a supply ship. If any shooting started, Mallorys' patrons didn't want to get caught in the cross fire.

Most of the crowd probably desired nothing more complex than companionship or peace; or maybe satisfaction for their guesses about what was going on. That night was a bad one for quiet, however.

Angus and Morn looked much the same as usual, as unsuited to each other as ever. Still they emitted an expectant tension which affected everyone around them, making calm men uneasy and uneasy men nervous. Angus glowered violence at anybody who crossed his gaze; blood from his swollen lip marked his chin. Pale, blank, and unsure, Morn held herself like a coiled spring, restrained only by willpower and circumstance from doing something wild.

The mood in Mallorys thickened steadily around them.

Then Nick Succorso and some of his people came in.

He was in a cheerful humor, laughing and joking, but no one was reassured. The way he ignored Angus and Morn didn't make anybody relax: the scars under his eyes were too dark. Something was going to happen.

The people who didn't wish to know what that was, left as inconspicuously as possible. Everyone else got ready for sudden movements.

When Security broke into the bar, some of the observers were surprised. The ones who'd probed a bit below the surface and thought they knew what was going on weren't.

Tables and chairs clattered back hastily: people milled around, jeering, cheering, trying to clear the way: a squad of guards drove into the confusion as fast as they could, determined to get their hands on Angus before he escaped.

So quickly that most people didn't see her do it, Morn Hyland left him and started through the crowd in Nick's direction.

But Angus was braced for her flight. He had good reflexes, and fear made him fast. This was the reason he'd brought her to Mallorys, the moment on which his life depended. He was a coward; and like a coward, he wanted to go on living even though his heart was broken. He hardly saw Security: he took note of the confusion around him only as a screen for his own actions.

Quick as a snake, he caught Morn by the wrist.

She struggled as well as she could. He was too strong. While she thrashed against his grip, she looked at him: the loathing and fright in her face were as loud as screams. Or maybe what she felt was incomprehension; maybe she thought he'd decided on a particularly brutal form of suicide. She'd been hoping, pleading, aching for an escape with every gram of her spirit—and now he'd caught her.

If he didn't release her—

He wanted to say something, but there were no words for it. And no time. His doom gathered against him. Security charged in from the door: Nick and his crew thrust forward from the other side, wedging a path for Morn through the crowd.

Holding her by the wrist, he slipped the control to her zone implant into her hand.

"I accept. The deal you offered. I'll cover you.

"Remember," he hissed as if he were pleading with her, *begging* her, "I could have killed you. I could have killed you anytime."

Then he let her go.

For a second, her eyes flared, and she stared at him.

During that moment, she seemed to understand him. Recognition passed between them. He had brought her here for this. To let her go. To give her what she wanted. And to ask her to spare his life.

Inside himself, he was stark naked with terror.

She had only a second to make her choice. Then Nick's people reached her, snatched her away.

But by that time she'd already shoved the zone-implant control like a small piece of immortality into one of her pockets, where no one could see it and take it to use against Angus Thermopyle.

Or against Morn herself.

After that, she was gone.

CHAPTER 18

So the fair maiden was rescued. The swashbuckling pirate bore her away with all her beauty, and her tormentor was left to pay the price of his crimes.

Angus was convicted of nothing more than stealing Station supplies. The evidence of *Bright Beauty*'s datacore was curiously imprecise. And the techs who examined *Starmaster* couldn't find any indication that the UMCP ship did anything except blow herself up; whether by sabotage or self-destruct was unclear. Without Morn's testimony, nothing else could be proved against Angus Thermopyle. Nevertheless that was enough to put him in lockup for the rest of his life.

Morn must have had an easier time with Nick than with Angus. Almost certainly he would have treated her better than Angus did—especially if he knew nothing, or could never be sure, about the zone implant. With the control in her own hands, she was effectively as free as if the implant had been removed. A timer and a little common sense made it possible for her to take care of her own gap-sickness.

The fact that he'd rescued her so cleverly only enhanced Nick Succorso's reputation. The way he'd framed Angus was too perfect to be criticized. After all, the Station recovered its supplies. And the arrival of the real supply ship on schedule revealed just how clever Nick had been.

The real story, however, was that Angus never complained he'd been framed. He never mentioned there was a traitor in Security; he made no effort to defend himself. For the most part, he betrayed no reaction at all to his doom. When he heard *Bright Beauty* was going to be dismantled, he howled as if he were in agony; but he let Morn and Nick go. He had that much courage, anyway.

Despite his horror of imprisonment, he was condemned to stay in lockup until he rotted.

This is the end of
*The Real Story.*
The story continues in
*The Gap into Vision:*
*Forbidden Knowledge.*

# AFTERWORD

Most writers hate the question, "Where do you get your ideas?"

This is because the answer tends to be at once ineffably mysterious and excruciatingly mundane. We are all in love with the magic of the imagination—otherwise we wouldn't be able to survive as creative artists—but none of us can explain how it works. In a sense, writers don't get ideas: ideas get writers. They happen to us. If we don't submit to their power, we lose them; so by trying to control or censor them we can make the negative choice of encouraging them to leave us alone. But we can never *force* ourselves to be truly creative. The best we can do is to teach ourselves receptiveness—and trust that ideas will come.

However, once the magic of the imagination has been accepted as given, any specific answer to the question often becomes almost violently anti-creative: for instance, "Well, I got that particular idea off a can of Lysol disinfectant in the men's room at Circle K." (I'm not making this up. One of the strongest scenes in *The Power that Preserves* was triggered in my head by a can of Lysol disinfectant in a men's room.) Such an answer may be perfectly accurate, but who wants to say it out loud? In these cases, the concrete source of the idea seems to demean its underlying imaginative magic. Hence the apparently arrogant or dismissive answers which writers have been giving ever since readers began asking the question.

But occasionally one or another of us is able to offer a practical answer without experiencing too much dissonance between what we say and how we feel about what we're saying. This *Afterword* is a case in point. I can discuss the sources and development for the sequence of four novels which follows directly after *The Real Story* while suffering no more severe distress than a blind astonishment that my mind works so *slowly*.

For some reason, a fair number of my best stories arise, not from one idea, but from two. In these cases, one idea comes first; it excites me enough to stay with me; yet despite its apparent (to me) potential, it stubbornly refuses to grow. Rather than expanding to take on character, event, and context, it simply sits in my head—often for many years—saying over and over again, "*Look* at me, you idiot. If you just *looked* at me, you would know what to do with me." Well, I *do* look; but I can't see what I need—until the first idea is intersected by the second. And then: Step back, boys and girls. She's a gusher.

I've heard Brian Aldiss talk about the same phenomenon. For him, a novel often requires two ideas. He describes them as a combination of "the familiar" and "the exotic." He begins with "the familiar"—usually something germane to his personal life, either thematically or experientially—but he can't write about it until "the familiar" is impacted by "the exotic." In his case, "the exotic" is usually a science fictional setting in which "the familiar" can play itself out: "the exotic" provides him with a stage on which he can dramatize "the familiar." Rather like a binary poison—or a magic potion—two inert elements combine to produce something of frightening potency.

The same dynamic works in reverse for me. I start with "the exotic" (remember that these are Aldiss's terms, not mine), but that idea declines to turn into a story until it is catalysed by "the familiar."

For example: *The Chronicles of Thomas Covenant* is squarely—and solely—founded on two ideas: unbelief and leprosy. The notion of writing a fantasy about an "unbeliever," a man who rejects the whole concept of fantasy, first came to me near the end of 1969. But the germ was dormant: no matter how I labored over it, I couldn't make it grow. Until I realized, in May of 1972, that my "unbeliever" should be a leper. As soon as those two ideas came together, my brain took fire. I spent the next three months feverishly taking notes, drawing maps, envisioning characters; studying the implications of unbelief and leprosy. Then I began writing.

This dynamic reverses Aldiss's because leprosy represented "the familiar" rather than "the exotic." I'd never written fantasy before: The whole concept of writing a fantasy about an "unbeliever" was exotic. However, thanks to the fact that my father was an orthopedic surgeon in India for twenty-one years, I was accustomed to leprosy on a variety of levels.

In the case of the four novels which ensue from *The Real Story*, the two ideas might be labelled "Angus Thermopyle" and "Richard Wagner."

Contrary to what one might expect, Angus represents "the familiar."


I wrote the first draft of *The Real Story* in the summer of 1985. At the time, I thought I was simply writing a novella: The idea came to me, so I worked on it at my earliest opportunity.

(Where did *that* idea come from? Well, this is a little embarrassing. It grew entirely out of the names of the characters. Driving through Albuquerque one day, I suddenly found myself chanting like a mantra, "Angus Thermopyle. Angus Thermopyle." I couldn't begin to guess why that name had appeared; but I could feel its importance, so I kept on chanting it. For weeks. And then, as if accidentally, another name manifested itself: Morn Hyland. So I chanted, "Angus Thermopyle," and, "Morn Hyland"—until they were joined by Nick Succorso. By this time, I liked the names so much that I began consciously trying to pull together a story good enough for them.)

My original intentions were explicitly archetypal. What I had in mind was an aesthetically perfect variation on *the* basic three-sided story: the story in which a Victim (Morn), a Villain (Angus), and a Rescuer (Nick) all change roles. (This, incidentally, is the essential difference between melodrama and drama. Melodrama presents a Victim, a Villain, and a Rescuer. Drama offers the same characters and then studies the process by which they change roles.) Victimized by Angus, Morn is rescued by Nick—but that, of course, is not the *real* story. The *real* story has to do with the way in which Nick becomes Angus's victimizer and Morn becomes Angus's rescuer.

When I'd finished the first draft of the novella, however, I found myself in a state of acute distress, for at least three reasons—only two of which were conscious. First, I realized immediately that what I'd written was by no means "aesthetically perfect." My work had fallen below my original intentions rather farther than usual. I'd planned a balanced triangle, with equal attention paid to each character and equal emphasis placed on each shifting role. But in practice I was unable to produce that balance.

Put simply, the problem was that Angus had taken over the story. Vital and malign, he dominated the narrative, reducing Morn to a shadow—and Nick to a cypher. In some ways, this made sense: as long as the action was viewed from Angus's point of view, Morn's motivations were unknowable, and Nick's were unimportant. But the result was that I'd written an intensive study of Angus's movement from Villain to Victim; but I'd only sketched in Morn's shift from Victim to Rescuer; and I hadn't paid any attention at all to Nick's change from Rescuer to Villain.

(If I weren't so damn *slow,* this would have given me a powerful clue to the third, unconscious reason for my distress.)

I was quite disappointed in myself.

Yet I was also aware of another reason for my distress. Unlike any other character I'd ever created, Angus made me feel *exposed.* It was as if in imagining him I'd tapped directly into the dark side of my own nature; as if I'd found him inside myself instead of inventing him. (In Aldiss's terms, he was "the familiar.") And that in turn shamed me. I felt irrationally sure that anyone who read *The Real Story* would see the "real" me, recognize the truth, and be disgusted.

Because I was ashamed of the novella, both artistically and personally, I decided not to publish it. At the time, I believed that I would never publish it.

Well, time works wonders. Among other things, it gives us the chance to think. And after I'd thought for a while, I began trying to do something about my shame.

There was nothing to be done about my personal shame, of course. I could only dismiss it. Time and thought brought me to the realization that I had no reason to feel ashamed. Suppose for a moment that my worst fears were realistic: that I am in fact an Angus Thermopyle thinly disgused by niceness; that this fact is transparent in *The Real Story;* and that all right-thinking readers will be disgusted by the results. So what? None of that impinges on the integrity of *The Real Story* itself. If I drew on some buried part of myself to create Angus, so much the better: at least I'm writing what I know. In any case, the crucial question for any artist is not: What are people going to think of me? It is: Have I given my best to my work? Nothing else matters.

Where *The Real Story* was concerned, I had to answer, "Yes and no." Yes, I was doing exactly what I'm supposed to do when I wrote the novella: I accepted the idea of "Angus" for the simple and sufficient reason that it came to me; I followed the idea where it chose to lead me, rather than trying to make it serve my own purposes. And no, I hadn't given my best to the work: I hadn't done everything in my power to raise the aesthetic level of the novella as high as possible.

So I spent the next two years, off and on, rewriting *The Real Story.* Indeed, I put it through my word processor at least six different times, developing and focusing Morn, enhancing Nick. And eventually I came to the conclusion that I was never going to be able to make it "aesthetically perfect." Judged by the standard of my original intentions, this book would always be a failure. For me as a writer, the effort of dealing with Angus was so urgent and compulsory that I couldn't treat Morn and Nick as his equals. What we might call the spatial constraints of the narrative didn't leave enough room for them.

(There it was again: a clue to the third, unconscious reason for my distress. But I still didn't recognize the truth.)

Fortunately, I was saved from the belief that *The Real Story* was doomed to artistic failure by what Dr. Who refers to as "lateral thinking." If you have an unscalable cliff in front of you and an unbeatable monster behind you, go sideways. Obedient to that dictum, I began to ask myself, not, "How did I go wrong within the novella?" but, "Where did I go wrong in my original intentions?"

Where, indeed? Well, where else? *The Real Story* was based on only one idea—and a *fair number of my best stories arise, not from one idea, but from two*. My problems with the book resulted from the need for a second idea.

However, I've told *this* story backward. *The Real Story* was actually the second idea, not the first. When I combined it with another idea which had already been in my head—alive, exciting, and totally static—for twenty years, I had a gusher.

> The real story, however, was that Angus never complained he'd been framed. He never mentioned there was a traitor in Security; he made no effort to defend himself. For the most part, he betrayed no reaction at all to his doom. When he heard *Bright Beauty* was going to be dismantled, he howled as if he were in agony; but he let Morn and Nick go. He had that much courage, anyway.
>
> Despite his horror of imprisonment, he was condemned to stay in lockup until he rotted.

So ends *The Real Story*. There's no indication here, certainly, that events will take four more books to run their course—or that the course they run will be epic in the Wagnerian sense; as large-scaled, intense, and ambitious as anything in *The Chronicles of Thomas Covenant*. That's because the original source for this sequence of novels was a recording of Richard Wagner's *Götterdammerung* (*The Twilight of the Gods*); the true genesis began in the fall of 1966.

That recording, which I purchased in September of 1966, wasn't my first experience with Wagner; but it was my first taste of Wagner's four-part opera cycle, *Der Ring des Nibelungen* (*The Ring of the Nibelung*), and it inspired me to purchase as quickly as my finances permitted (I spent three years saving pennies) recordings of the other three parts of *The Ring: Das Rheingold* (*The Rhine Gold*), *Die Walküre* (*The Valkyrie*), and *Siegfried* (no translation necessary). In a relatively short time, I knew that I'd discovered my musical alter-ego—a kind of transcendental *dopplegänger*. Wagner's music inspired me. (Indeed, some of the literary techniques of *The Chronicles of Thomas Covenant* were extrapolated from the way Wagner used musical ideas.) And the story of *The Ring*—especially in the twin climaxes of *The Valkyrie* and *The Twilight of the Gods*—moved me as deeply as any story I've ever encountered.

Soon after I fell in love with *The Ring,* I conceived the ambition of writing a sequence of novels based on Wagner's epic.

My intentions were conceptual rather than literal. I wasn't interested in simply retelling the story of Wotan's doomed struggle to preserve the power of the gods in the face of pressure from giants, dwarves, and humankind. Rather I wanted to create an analogue which would allow me to explore the same themes and exigencies on my own terms. Most particularly, I was fascinated by Wotan himself, who finds that an understanding of his own power leads to the destruction of that power, as well as of himself and everything he represents; even more, that an understanding of his power leads him to *will* his own destruction.

But the idea remained utterly and entirely static—until 1987, when I realized that the world of Angus, Morn, and Nick offered me the perfect setting for the story I had in mind.

(In addition, of course, I realized that using *The Real Story* to launch a larger narrative gave me a perfect opportunity to make constructive use of the ways in which it didn't measure up to my original intentions. The relative imbalance of the roles in the novella becomes a strength rather than a weakness when its implications can be pursued in subsequent books. *This* was the third, unconscious reason for my distress concerning *The Real Story*. My work there disturbed me because it wasn't *complete*—and couldn't be completed without the catalysis of a second idea.)

As the ending of *The Real Story* suggests, the relevance of Wagner's epic to Angus's fate may not be readily apparent. That's the only excuse I can offer for my slowness to comprehend that Wagner and Angus needed each other.

Fortunately or unfortunately, depending on whether afterwords are considered a pleasure or an affliction, I can't explain the relevance without discussing *The Ring* in some detail.

Put simply, Wagner's opera cycle tells the story of how the gods were brought down by two things: a bitter curse; and an act of unselfish heroism.

### Das Rheingold

In a world where humankind is the weakest and least effective form of life, the gods (Wotan; Fricka, his wife, goddess of family and hearth; Donner, god of storm; Froh, god of light; Loge, god of fire; and Freia, goddess of eternal life) rule proudly—although they are neither the oldest nor the most potent forces or beings in their sphere. However, their power is precarious: It depends on their ability to compel submission from two magical and creative races, the giants (builders of large things) and the dwarves (builders of small things), both of which aspire to supplant the gods. Hungry for supremacy, Wotan has carved a staff from the World Tree; and into his staff he cuts the bargains and treaties he makes to consolidate his dominance, so that his authority becomes part of the natural order. But precisely because his rule is based on authority and law rather than on love or virtue, it inspires resentment. So, to make himself and the gods secure, he cuts a deal with the giants to build an impregnable fortress for him: Valhalla. His idea is to fill Valhalla with heroes to fight for him, so that he can resist any challenge from either giants or dwarves.

Two problems arise immediately, however: one of his own making, one outside his control.

The one he can't control involves three watery females, the Rhine Maidens, and a dwarf, Alberich, who falls in lust with them. (Alright, I admit it: I've never found the Rhine Maidens themselves especially convincing.) The Maidens were fathered by one of the aforementioned older beings, and their purpose in life (or at least in the Rhine) is to guard the Rhine Gold, one of the archetypal sources of power (like the World Tree). Now, the secret of the Rhine Gold is this: Any being who "foreswears love," giving up all bonds of passion or commitment, takes the Gold, and forges it into a ring, will gain the power to impose his will on others. This the Maidens gleefully reveal to Alberich, primarily because they think his lust—and loneliness—are funny. (Characters with nothing better to do in a story than sit around being archetypal are often rather insensitive.)

But they underestimate the scale of his loneliness and desire. Taunted past bearing by beauties he cannot have, he does indeed foreswear love, take the Gold, and forge it into a ring. Before anyone notices what he's up to, he gains dominion over all the dwarves, accumulates a vast treasure—and commences to plan his attack on the gods. Thus begins an evil which can only be ended by returning the Gold to the Maidens.

The problem Wotan could have avoided, if he were wiser—i.e., less hungry for power—is that for the sake of getting Valhalla built "on the cheap" he has made a bargain with the giants which he has no intention of keeping: He has offered them Freia (source of the gods' immortality) in exchange for the fortress. This is manifestly misguided, since his supremacy depends on bargains and agreements; but he is young, strong, and arrogant—and he believes that once Valhalla is built he'll be able to persuade the giants to accept some other payment.

No such luck. The giants want *Freia,* or to hell with Valhalla and the gods. (They realize, of course, that without her the gods can't endure; so their insistence on correct payment is inspired by a desire to bring Wotan down.)

This is a terrible moment for Wotan—he's doomed if he breaks his bargain, and doomed if he keeps it—but he isn't yet wise enough to realize the full implications. Instead of facing up to the consequences of his own actions, he hits upon a solution of convenience. Maybe the giants will accept Alberich's treasure (and ring) as payment in Freia's place. The giants agree: they've heard about the ring.

At this point, Alberich's only weakness is that he isn't yet accustomed to the sheer size of his new power. He doesn't really understand that he stands on the brink of godhood himself: He's too busy enjoying his treasure—and his ability to torture his own people with impunity. In consequence, he's vulnerable, not to force, but to trickery. Helped by the cunning of Loge, Wotan obtains the ring by subterfuge and immediately uses it to master both Alberich and the treasure.

This would be a self-destructive act on Wotan's part in any case: He has no right to the ring, but he is immediately consumed by desire for its power. However, his position deteriorates further when Alberich curses the ring. Only in losing the ring does Alberich grasp its magnitude. In an apotheosis of grief and rage, he cries:

As its gold gave me power without limit,
now let its magic bring death to whoever wears it.
No happy man shall be glad of it,
no fortunate man know the smile of its bright gleam.
Whoever possess it shall be seared by anxiety,
and whoever has it not, shall be nagged by envy.
Everyone shall hanker for its possession
but no one enjoy it to advantage.
Without gain its master shall guard it,
for it draws him to his assassin.
Condemned to death the coward will be in fear's grip.
As long as he lives he shall long for death,
the ring's master be slave to the ring. . . .

Now Wotan is in *real* trouble. The ring is cursed, but he desires it too much to give it up. Yet it is the only payment the giants will accept in Freia's place. Without her, the gods must die. Wotan can't simply declare war on the giants because the enforcement of his bargains is carved into his staff, the source of his power: to violate his own commitments will undo him. And the natural order of existence can only be restored by returning the Gold to the Rhine Maidens—which will force Freia into the hands of the giants.

At last Wotan begins to understand his plight. With a little help from Erda, the Earth Mother (another of those preexisting beings), he gains enough insight to realize that he must surrender the ring. So the giants take the ring; Freia remains with the gods; and Wotan gets Valhalla.

Alas, this is only a stop-gap resolution. The natural order is still in jeopardy. The ring remains a threat to the gods. And the curse *works*: The giants proceed to slaughter each other until only one remains to hold the ring; and that one sequesters himself (as a dragon), dedicating his entire being to the simple goal of preventing anyone from getting the ring away from him.

### Die Walküre

Wotan is now obsessed with understanding his dilemma. After some intensive study with Erda (study which just happens to produce eight daughters—the Valkyries), he learns that the only cure for the evil of the ring is to return the Gold to the Maidens. Unfortunately, he can't do that: He can't get the ring away from the dragon without breaking his bargain with the giants. However, in due course he hits on the only apparent solution to the problem: He decides to use an agent to obtain the ring for him.

First, on a human woman he gets himself a son, Siegmund (and, not coincidentally, a daughter as well, Sieglinde, Siegmund's twin). Then he trains his son to be strong, brave, and *desperate* enough to tackle a dragon. Sadly, this training involves separating Siegmund and Sieglinde and abandoning them both to lives of extreme loneliness, abuse, and danger. Neither of them has any idea that their father loves them—and needs them. All they know of life is bitter survival against cruel odds.

Too bad. Wotan's plan was flawed from the beginning—a fact that becomes transparent when Siegmund and Sieglinde find each other and fall in love (she gets pregnant). This attracts the attention of Fricka: As goddess of matrimony, she's responsible for punishing sins like incest. She forces Wotan to recognize that any agent of his is no different from him; that for Siegmund to get the ring will be the same as if Wotan himself took it. Therefore Wotan can't use Siegmund to solve his problems for him; and so he has no defense against Fricka's argument that Siegmund and Sieglinde must die for their crime. Broken-hearted—and aware of his own doom—Wotan commands his favorite Valkyrie, Brünnhilde, to make sure that Sieg-mund and Sieglinde are killed by Hunding, Sieglinde's rapist/hus-band.

It is Brünnhilde's act of unselfish heroism which changes the nature of the dilemma.

As Wotan's favorite, she thinks of herself as his will incarnate. However, his pain when he condemns Siegmund and Sieglinde moves her deeply. And she is further distraught by Siegmund's passionate and fatal loyalty to Sieglinde. At the last, the Valkyrie chooses not to help Hunding execute Siegmund. Instead, she fights for Siegmund against Hunding, directly defying Wotan, the All-Father.

Outraged, Wotan intervenes personally, killing both Siegmund and Hunding. In the confusion, however, Brünnhilde escapes with Sieglinde. If Siegmund cannot be saved, perhaps his son can be preserved. She helps Sieglinde flee into a trackless forest (the same forest, incidentally, where the dragon guards his treasure), then turns to face Wotan's wrath (thereby buying Sieglinde time to run).

Because she has opposed him, Wotan condemns Brünnhilde to an enchanted sleep, from which she can only be awakened by the shame of being "taken" as a mortal's lover. And because he loves her, he guards her sleep with a fire which will prevent any man who isn't utterly fearless from approaching her.

### Siegfried

Sieglinde, meanwhile, struggles on into the forest. Close to death, she comes upon a cave where Mime, Alberich's brother, has been living ever since Alberich's hold over the dwarves was broken. Mime keeps her alive until her son, Siegfried, is born; after she dies in childbirth, he raises young Siegfried with one goal in mind: to make Siegfried utterly fearless so that he'll be brave enough to fight the dragon and get the ring for his foster father.

Like most plans in this story, Mime's proves flawed. For one thing, both Wotan and Alberich know what he's doing—and Alberich has plans of his own. For another, Mime succeeds only too well: He teaches Siegfried to be *so* fearless that Siegfried can't stand the sight of his craven foster father and won't do anything for the dwarf. Trying to trick him, Mime tells Siegfried he'll learn something wonderful—fear—if he meets the dragon; so Siegfried decides to accept the adventure, despite his loathing for Mime. But this, too, doesn't work out well for poor Mime.

Instead of learning fear, Siegfried kills the dragon (laughing all the way) and gets the ring; in addition, he captures a magic talisman, the tarnhelm, which makes him a shape-changer, and gains from the dragon's blood the ability to understand birds. At once, a bird tells him that Mime is about to poison him. In righteous indignation, Siegfried kills Mime. Then the bird tells him about Brünnhilde. Hungry for more adventures, he goes off to rescue her.

Along the way, he encounters Wotan, who forbids him to approach the magic fire. But Siegfried is nothing if not self-willed: Oblivious to symbolism, he breaks Wotan's spear and continues his quest to rescue the enchanted woman.

(Without his spear, of course, Wotan is finished. In fact, he had reason to believe that his spear wouldn't stop the boy. His decision to challenge Siegfried regardless is complex. On the one hand, he knows that if his spear can't stop Siegfried the gods are doomed anyway: They'll never be able to control whatever use is made of the ring. On the other, he understands that unless his spear—his rule—is shattered, the world will never be free of the destructive effects of his bargains. He challenges Siegfried in an attempt to simultaneously save and destroy himself.)

## Götterdammerung

In a manner of speaking, Siegfried is a dream come true for Brünnhilde—a mortal so heroic that he might as well be a god. She gives him her heart, as well as a spell to protect him from any danger as long as he doesn't turn his back on it; and he goes out into the world to have more adventures so that she'll be proud of him. (I should perhaps have mentioned earlier that Siegfried isn't very bright.)

Almost immediately, he finds himself in the domain of the Gibichungs, a human tribe with failed ambitions and an imprecise moral sense. They are led by Gunther, unwed; his spinster sister, Gutrune; and his half-brother, Hagan (Alberich's son and agent). The Gibichungs want glory through Siegfried; Hagan wants the ring. Toward those ends, they conspire to give Siegfried a potion which causes him to forget Brünnhilde. Then they send him to obtain Brünnhilde for Gunther (using the tarnhelm to appear as Gunther), for which his reward will be Gutrune's hand in marriage. (This only works becaue Siegfried can't remember ever meeting another woman, so to him Gutrune looks good.)

When Brünnhilde is brought from the safety of her magic fire and given to Gunther, she is quite understandably outraged by Siegfried's apparent betrayal. She denounces him furiously. Hagan promptly gives Siegfried another potion which causes him to re-member Brünnhilde and forget Gutrune; and as soon as Siegfried unselfconsciously admits the substantial accuracy of Brünnhilde's denunciation, Hagan claims that revelation as an excuse to spear Siegfried in the back.

Even in death, however, Siegfried is so strong that no one can get the ring away from him. And Brünnhilde is at last able to see the truth of his behavior. To honor him, she commands a funeral pyre and joins him on it. As soon as fire melts the ring, the Rhine

Maidens are able to reclaim their gold. The story ends with the natural order restored—and Valhalla burning in the background. So the gods are brought to an end, and humankind is freed from arbitrary external dominance to work out its own destiny.

(The logic here is profound, yet difficult to explain. Once Wotan's spear was broken, the gods were, in effect, kept alive by the force of Alberich's curse. They couldn't die: The holder of the ring could be murdered, but everyone else who fell under the curse was compelled to yearn and suffer helplessly, as long as the ring—and therefore the curse—endured.)

So what, one might well ask, does all this have to do with ore piracy and space stations?

The answer is simple enough, as long as another, more concrete question is answered first. If Angus Thermopyle is a pirate who preys on human miners and shipping, to whom does he sell his booty? Ore isn't cash, after all: It's relatively useless unless it can be processed. And ore processing is capital intensive. Pirates like Angus and Nick would never exist—and the UMCP in turn would have no mandate to combat them—unless they had a market for their ill-gotten gains. So what kind of world lies behind *The Real Story*? Is humankind publicly divided against itself? Or is it in conflict with something else; something anti-human? Doesn't the UMCP mandate against piracy derive its moral authority from the fact that the pirates are, in effect, selling out humankind?

Once such questions have been asked (in the context of *Der Ring des Nibelungen*), the step from *The Real Story* to the next book, *Forbidden Knowledge,* is a small one. As soon as I began to think of the UMCP as legal gods threatened by the science fiction equivalent of shape-changing dwarves, I could hardly stop before I reached the wonderfully perverse notion of Angus and Morn as Siegmund and Sieglinde. And after that, as I've already indicated, my story became a gusher.

However, imagining Angus and Morn as Siegmund and Sieglinde suggests just how fundamentally non-literal my use of *The Ring* is. *The Ring* is not my story: It is one of the seeds from which my story grew. In several ways, I've moved a considerable distance from my source.

For one thing, there are themes in Wagner that I don't want to pursue. His work contains a kind of structural sexism which leaves me cold. (The Rhine Maidens make me think of the scene in *Monty Python and the Holy Grail* where a peasant shouts at Arthur, "You can't wield supreme executive power just because some watery tart pitched a sword at you!") And I don't respond to characters whose power derives from their "innocence": To my mind, Siegfried is untrammeled by fear, not because of his innocence, but because he's too stupid to live. Wagner's idea that knowledge paralyzes power seems inadequate to me—witness the entire *Chronicles of Thomas Covenant*.

For another, "Angus Thermopyle" alters the essential terms and possibilities of "Richard Wagner." In a sense, setting *is* story—and the setting of *The Real Story* is science fictional rather than mythopoeic. Almost by definition, the conflicts of the story now become political rather than archetypal. Of necessity, every valence of *The Ring* is transformed. The most obvious result is that the onus of the story shifts from gods and dwarves to human beings. If human life in space is to be preserved, it must be preserved, not by All-

Fathers and Valkyries, but by the descendants of the Gibichungs.

The consequences of this transformation are everywhere. Just to mention a few examples. My "gods" derive their ability to endure, not from immortality, but from their control over information. As a crime against the order which the UMCP is pledged to protect, incest would have no meaning; so there's no reason for Angus and Morn to be siblings. And I use no direct analogues to either Wotan's staff or Alberich's ring—although Angus's ability to edit datacores has interesting implications.

Yet *The Ring* is present in each of the four novels which follows *The Real Story*. When characters like Warden Dios, Min Donner, Godsen Frik, and Hashi Lebwohl take the stage, they come, as one might say, "trailing clouds of glory"—the ether of their Wagnerian avatars. And who better to represent the dwarves than the Amnion, who desire nothing less than the destruction of the natural existence of humanity?

Whether Angus and Morn can preserve their own humanity (not to mention their entire species) is a question which could only have arisen from the intersection of *The Real Story* and *Der Ring des Nibelungen*.